I0703037

Just One Surprise

The Billionaire Barons of Texas • Book Eleven

CHRIS KENISTON

Indie House Publishing

This book is a work of fiction. Names, characters, places and incidents are the product of the author's imagination or are used fictionally. Any resemblance to actual events, locales, or persons, living or dead, is coincidental.

Copyright 2024 Christine Baena
Print Edition

Indie House Publishing

MORE BOOKS
By Chris Keniston

The Billionaire Barons of Texas
Just One Date
Just One Spark
Just One Dance
Just One Take
Just One Taste
Just One Shot
Just One Chance
Just One Mistake
Just One Family
Just One Rodeo
Just One Surprise
Just One Look

Hart Land
Heather
Lily
Violet
Iris
Hyacinth
Rose
Calytrix
Zinnia
Poppy
Picture Perfect

Farraday Country
Adam
Brooks
Connor
Declan
Ethan

Finn
Grace
Hannah
Ian
Jamison
Keeping Eileen
Loving Chloe
Morgan
Neil
Owen
Paxton
Quinn

Honeymoon Series
Honeymoon for One
Honeymoon for Three
Honeymoon for Four
Honeymoon for Five
Honeymoon for Six
Honeymoon for Seven

Aloha Romance Series:
Aloha Texas
Almost Paradise
Mai Tai Marriage
Dive Into You
Look of Love
Love by Design
Love Walks In
Shell Game
Flirting with Paradise

Surf's Up Flirts:
(Aloha Series Companions)
Shall We Dance
Love on Tap
Head Over Heels
Perfect Match
Just One Kiss
It Had to Be You
Cat's Meow

CHAPTER ONE

"How did it go?" Cooper Baron's assistant Katrina crossed into his office.

"Same as always. I present the city with perfectly detailed plans and they want more."

Chuckling softly, Katrina shook her head. "Like you didn't know that was going to happen."

The woman was right. He'd been overly optimistic when he submitted the plans for the permits. "After all, I've only helped Rachel gut and rebuild more houses than the pencil pushers at city hall could count on all their hands and feet."

"I know." She crossed her arms. "How bad is it?"

He shook his head. "Not terribly. They want an additional cross-beam. I know it's not needed. You know it's not needed. And I suspect so does city hall, but nowadays it's all about CYA."

"We *have* become the most litigious society in the world."

"Lucky us." Tilting his drafting table another inch, he finished making the requested changes. Thankfully, Rachel didn't have the demolition on her latest project scheduled to start for another couple of weeks. That would be plenty of time to get city hall on board. Things were much easier before Chuck Nelson retired. After more than a decade working together, they'd developed a streamlined rapport. Now it looked like Cooper was going to be starting all over.

It also struck him that in this case, his last name had worked as a strike against him. Every once in a while—okay, more often than not—the Baron family name opened doors and cut through red tape. But sometimes it stirred resentment in folks who felt life had come too easily to anyone with that last name. He'd be an idiot to argue there weren't perks to being a Baron. The biggest perk had absolutely nothing to do with power or prestige and everything to do with the love and support of a very large family. Despite Baron Enterprises having its fingers in everything from hotel resorts and restaurant chains, to sports teams and venture projects, the family's best benefit was just that, family. Even though there were enough Baron grandchildren to form a small city, they all knew each other, played with each other, worked with each other, and loved each other. And more importantly, had each other's backs, no questions asked.

Of course, having a surly retired Marine for a grandfather posed its own challenges, but in the end, love and respect trumped it all.

"Any updates on the new project manager?" Katrina picked up a stack of folders from the outbox on his desk.

Yes, nowadays everything was electronic, but he believed in paper backups for almost everything. Probably his grandfather's fault. "Well, she hasn't changed her mind and run for the hills, if that's what you're asking."

"Last I heard she was either reporting for work this Thursday or next Monday."

He nodded. "Right. Her replacement seemed to have enough of a handle on all the work in progress so Tess will be able to start Thursday."

"Tess? I thought her name is Teresa?"

"Yeah." He couldn't stop the smile from crossing his lips at the memories of the strong-willed, confident and oh so stubborn freshman who tutored him through physics. After being laid up with mono for over a month, he'd fallen woefully behind in classes and physics was the only teacher that refused to give him a lick of assistance in catching up. Tess had come to the rescue. Though he had no idea if she still used the nickname he'd given her. When her name came across his desk on the short list for applicants, he didn't even bother with an interview; he just gave approval to hire her on the spot. If she was half as capable as the high school student he'd been so in awe of, she'd do a fantastic job for Baron Enterprises. "Teresa. That's right."

Katrina nodded. "Also, Gibbs from the Dallas hotel has been blowing up voicemail. Something about the new concrete supplier."

Immediately, Cooper checked his cell phone. "Dang it." Somehow, he'd switched his new phone to silent no vibration. The list of people who had been calling or texting him had him scrolling frantically. Words like 'honeycomb' and 'cracks' had Cooper biting down hard on his back teeth. All indicators of subpar concrete. "I'll call him now."

"You'll also want to call your grandfather."

Cooper blew out a sigh. "Did Gibbs reach out to the Governor?"

Lips pressed tightly, clutching the folders to her chest, Katrina bobbed her head.

"Great. I'll call Gibbs first, then the Governor." And then he'd deal with the other texts pinging his phone. No matter what else was going on, this just became a priority. Nothing with the Baron name attached to it will ever be done by cutting corners to save money. Nothing. Not. Ever. That was not, nor would it ever be, the Baron way.

"Knock knock." One of Teresa Gordon's associates rapped on the non-existent door of her corner cubicle.

That was just one of the small things she was looking forward to in her new job, a real office with a real door. "Hey, come on in."

Smiling, Ashley strolled in and came to a stop by Teresa's nearly empty desk. "Looks like you're almost done packing."

"Pretty much." Officially, yesterday had been her last day, but she'd opted to come in today to pack up the rest of her things, just in case her replacement had any last-minute questions. So far, the replacement seemed to be more than efficient enough.

"Remember, if there's a spot for me at Baron Enterprises; don't forget your favorite coworker."

Fully aware that her moving to Texas to work for a major player like Baron Enterprises made her the object of envy for many of the people in her office. She actually liked working with Ashley, regretted not making more time to build a friendship outside of the office, but starting a new job with a new infant and a major case of sleep deprivation, a social life hadn't been on her agenda. "You know I won't."

"I'll hold you to that. Baron Enterprises is the most employee-friendly outfit in the country. I'd move to Timbuktu for a job with Barons. My sister's friend is an admin with one of their subsidiaries and she got sixty days paid leave before her due date and another ninety days after the baby. And then, having daycare in the building, she was able to keep nursing."

Teresa nodded. That was just one of the many reasons she jumped at the chance to apply for a project management position with the Barons. Having Emma nearby would do wonders to ease her guilt at having to work for a living. Not worrying about taking time off when she got sick, not that she got sick that often, but knowing that her job was secure even if she put her daughter first was huge for her. Having a chance to work with the Barons again was just as sweet a part of the deal. Tutoring Cooper Baron all those years ago had been the springboard to a close friendship and spending time at the ranch, getting to know a good number of the family. She really loved his grandmother. A nicer woman did not exist. Once she got past the Governor's military demeanor, she found comfort in the frequent sparkle in the old man's eyes.

"Taking this?" Ashley held up Teresa's Employee of the Year award from a few years ago.

"Might be the only award I ever get." She took it from her friend and put it in the box with her other desktop items. How much would get unpacked was debatable, and she was very unlikely to display the thing at Barons. Maybe she'd win another. Did Barons even give out awards? Not that it mattered. While she'd definitely give her all to the job, there was a lot less 'all' available since she had Emma. She needed to keep it all in perspective.

Checking the drawers one last time, carefully opening and closing each one, then scanning the room, she wrapped her arms around the small box and straightened.

"So this is really it?" Ashley almost looked ready to cry.

"It's not like I'm moving to Bora Bora."

"At least if you were I'd have a good reason to visit."

The two women laughed.

"Texas is a short flight from Virginia." Not that she expected Ashley to actually fly to Texas when they'd not bothered to drive cross-town.

"You bet. Who knows, maybe I'll surprise you and Emma one day. Ashley shrugged. "They tell me there are lots of good-looking cowboys in Texas."

"There you go. Two reasons to visit." Laughing and walking down the hall, Teresa shifted the box to one hip the way she might carry her daughter, freeing one hand to wave back at a few people before reaching the elevator.

Inside, the trip down seemed slower than usual. She'd been looking forward to the possibilities with her new job, but right now, everything seemed so much more real. Thinking about all the changes coming to her and Emma's world, she couldn't stop smiling. Life was definitely looking up.

CHAPTER TWO

Hands on her hips, Teresa surveyed the living room. So much more space than her tiny apartment in Virginia. Already though, after hours of moving the furniture back and forth, she'd settled on the plan she liked best and determined when she was ready to house hunt to buy, she did not want a corner fireplace. When the house was empty, she thought the fireplace was adorable, until she'd moved in and tried to arrange furniture around it. For now, she was very content. Off to one side was a nook that most likely had been intended for a computer area or perhaps homework, but it was perfect for a toy area for Emma.

"More," Emma's voice carried from her high chair. The precious girl was talking up a storm lately. From time to time in almost full sentences. Teresa was going to hate it when those cute little communications were gone. Though she looked forward to hearing all about what was going on in that sweet baby's mind.

"More juice?"

"Yes." Emma waved her empty sippy cup at her mother.

"What's the magic word?"

"Peas."

Close enough. "One cup of juice coming up." Reaching into the fridge, she paused at how light the juice container felt. "Foo."

"Foo," Emma repeated.

Glancing at her daughter merrily grinning from her seat, Teresa was reminded once more that she needed to be seriously careful about what she said out loud. She also realized, in her determination to unpack quickly and make their new rental feel like a home, she'd overlooked her grocery list. Setting the cup on the tray, she took her daughter in for a moment. Big green eyes and dirty blonde hair, with a dimple on one cheek, her daughter flashed a smile that melted Teresa's heart every time. "Mama's going to get your shoes and we'll head out to the grocery store. We need more milk, and juice, and bacon."

"Bacon!" Emma shouted gleefully.

"Not now, sweetie. That's for breakfast tomorrow."

"Morrow."

"Yes," she couldn't not smile back at her daughter, "tomorrow."

Another second passed and Emma waved her hands by her ears, signaling *all done*. It had taken Teresa a bit to realize that her little girl had been picking up sign language from one of her language development television shows. So far Emma had taught her mother, *food*, *more*, and *all done*. Teresa had already known how to sign I love you, and every time she did it to Emma, the toddler would grin and whisper back, *Mama*!

In a new home, it took Teresa longer than usual to gather up socks and shoes for Emma, but once she had the baby all ready to go, Teresa grabbed her bag and keys and was out the door. Of course the question was where to go. Having moved to not just a new home and city, but a whole new state with a different staple of stores, she hadn't had time to scope out where to get groceries.

"Well, how do you like that?" Teresa glanced at her GPS, delighted to discover a major grocery chain only a couple of blocks away. At first, she thought perhaps it would be a good idea to drive around just a bit after picking up the groceries. Get a better idea of what's around, and let Emma enjoy the ride before naptime. Then it struck her that driving all around her new town of Spring in sweltering weather with milk in the car wasn't one of her finest ideas.

"Shall we take a short drive now?"

"Yes."

Glancing over, she watched Emma's reaction from the

camera screen. "Okay. Let's take a drive."

"Drive." Emma waved her favorite stuffed toy.

For the next short while, Teresa drove up and down the nearest major street, glancing left and right at traffic lights, occasionally taking a detour into one of the neighborhoods, pondering where she might want to actually buy a house. Of course, unlike this house that she rented based on the pretty street, mature trees, and ease of reaching the park and ride, she understood that the next move would be based on schools. Glancing over at the camera, soon it would be time to turn the car seat to forward facing. How had the last almost two years gone by so fast? Elementary school had seemed so far away when Emma was born, and now, it seemed to be creeping up too fast.

A horn tooted lightly behind her and she realized she'd been lost in thought and not paying attention to the light. Stepping quickly on the gas before the car honked again, she lurched forward only to hear a loud smacking sound seconds before she was spinning in the intersection. Emma let out a screeching cry, and Teresa shook her head to clear her mind, another bang came from the opposite side, sending her car sliding across the pavement. Her head snapped left then right, hit something hard and blinking she could hear Emma but the camera was gone.

Blinking again, the car seemed to be rocking, or was it spinning? "Emma," she called out, but her voice sounded too low even to her own ears, while Emma's crying grew louder. "It's, o-k-aye," she managed to force out before her voice drifted off and someone turned off all the lights.

Some days Cooper wondered why he bothered getting out of bed. What should have been the simplest of submissions had once again been nixed by the permit department in city hall. There was no missing when someone was messing with him merely because of who he was. If he'd been smart, he would have waited for Tess and have her go downtown as the project manager. Even though this was a Baron project, perhaps a different last name on the person delivering the plans would have rendered a better result.

"So now what?" Katrina stood over his shoulder.

"I add one more change to the design, then wait for Tess to start work and hand this off to her."

"Sounds like a plan." She dropped a file on his desk. "This is the report Gibbs sent. I went ahead and printed it off so you can highlight what stands out for you."

Stretching out his hand to draw the folder closer, he nodded. Katrina had worked with him long enough to know that despite being a member of the technology generation, he still liked to highlight and study on old-fashioned paper. Later he would convert his notes to a computer file. "As soon as Tess starts, we'll get her in the loop. What I'm hearing from Gibbs isn't jiving with the referrals. This company has a stellar reputation."

The phone in Katrina's adjoining office rang. "Excuse me." Hurrying away, her heels clacking on the hardwood floor, Katrina reached across her desk to answer the phone. Another minute and she dinged his speaker. "You'd better take this call. It's County Hospital."

His heart started bouncing in his chest, slamming against his ribs. Reaching for the phone, his mind ran through a long list of who could be hurt: his grandfather, or grandmother, or mom and dad, or any of his siblings, or cousins. Stabbing at the phone, he didn't bother stalling. "Hello."

"Cooper Baron?"

"Yes."

"Oh, good. Then you know Teresa Gordon?"

"I do."

"You'd better hurry down. There's been an accident."

Accident. "Is she all right?"

"The doctors will explain when you arrive."

"On my way." Already on his feet, he stepped back, dropped the phone into the cradle and crossed the room in only a few long strides. Pausing just long enough to lean into Katrina's office. "Teresa's been in an accident. I'm on my way to County."

Katrina looked up from her screen. "Is it serious?"

"They didn't say."

"Keep us posted, please."

With a curt nod, he turned on his heel and rushed out of the building. The first thing to come to mind was why the heck was the hospital calling him? Surely she had someone closer, someone who had seen her in the last ten years. Of course, when he'd known her she'd been in the foster system. An only child, there was little surprise she didn't have a lot of family, or any family, but surely she had someone? He probably broke several traffic laws including a few orange lights, as his grandmother called them, but he made it to the ER in record time.

Trotting across the parking lot, he hurried into the building, immediately scanning the signs for the reception desk. Spotting the young woman clacking away at the keyboard, he pivoted and rushed to her. "Someone called me and told me to hurry down. I'm here for Teresa Gordon?"

It took a very long moment before she stopped typing and looked up. "Your name?"

"Cooper Baron."

One brow lifted as she returned to typing, then nodded and pointed over her shoulder. "If you'll go through those double doors, someone inside will direct you and bring you up to date."

Never before had he had to rush to the ER for anyone. It suddenly struck him how blessed he'd been, and how worried he was for a woman he had not seen in at least a decade. Stopping at another desk, he looked from one person to another before interrupting. "I'm here for Teresa Gordon."

A brunette seated in front of a computer pushed to her feet and gestured for him to follow her. "You're just in time. We were wondering when someone was going to show up."

"How is she?"

"Not good. Someone ran a red light, t-boned her car.

She's yet to regain consciousness. There seems to be some internal bleeding. She's about to head into surgery. A few more minutes and you'd have missed her." The woman drew back a faded blue curtain and for a brief moment Cooper's heart stopped.

White as a sheet, Teresa didn't look anything like the bright young woman he remembered. Visions of his Princess Tess giggling over ice cream at the Alamode as she tried to get his thick head to absorb basic physics principles, or her long dark hair bouncing in a ponytail as she trotted down the steps of Keaton hall, flashed in contrast to the woman lying in bed now. The memory squeezed at his heart. Her shoulder length chestnut hair was pushed back and clumps of dry blood still painted several strands surrounding a white bandage along her temple. "Head injury?"

"There doesn't appear to be anything serious. No sign of brain swelling."

"Then why is she unconscious?"

"She's pretty banged up. Sometimes it's just nature's way of helping the body heal."

Before he could think of another question, two men came up beside him. Moving IV bags, and other equipment, without thinking, he snatched her untethered hand. "You've got this, Tess."

Another moment and one orderly cleared his throat. "We need to get her to surgery."

"Of course." Forcing himself to release his grip on her, he took a step in retreat. In a flash they had her on her way out of the ER.

His gaze lingered on the disappearing gurney. As crazy as it sounded, his heart ached for the sweet young girl who had become a confidant and his best cheerleader in high school.

"Mr. Gordon?" A young man holding a small box came to a stop by the nurse.

"Baron," he clarified. "Cooper Baron."

"Oh. Sorry. Here are Miss Gordon's personal belongings."

He stared into the box he'd been handed. A shoulder strap handbag, a small plastic bag with a few pieces of jewelry, and a cell phone with a smashed screen didn't take up much space.

He must have looked more than a little stunned as the first nurse lightly touched his arm. "The doctor is very optimistic."

Optimistic? The words internal bleeding came rushing back to the forefront of his mind. Surely there must be someone else who needed to be called. He'd have Katrina check who her emergency contact was on the paperwork she'd given to personnel. In the meantime, it looked like he was responsible for Teresa's belongings.

"If you'd like to put that in your car, then you can head up to the fifth floor."

"The waiting room?"

"Pediatrics. It was the best place for your daughter."

His what?

CHAPTER THREE

Cooper had never considered himself slow to catch on, but right about now he was totally baffled. He had not seen Teresa Gordon since she left for college on the east coast, and by the time she'd graduated they'd drifted apart completely. Why would anyone think he was the father of her child?

"We were afraid that she'd have to go with Social Services if we didn't find the father." The same nurse held a tablet in her hand, scrolling through pages as she spoke.

The words Social Services jumped out at him. Tess would hate any child of hers being turned over to the same system she'd lived in for most of her young life. Hate it. But could it be any worse than turning the child over to a confirmed bachelor with zero experience?

What was he thinking? He can't do this, and he certainly can't let the hospital believe he's the father. Surely, there was fraud or other legal issues that would arise from that crazy lie.

"Oh, Sandy," the same nurse called to a woman strolling past them. "Can you take Mr. Baron up to pediatrics, please? He's here for his daughter, little Emma."

"Oh, you found him." The woman smiled up at him. From her apron-like uniform, he suspected she was a volunteer and not a nurse. "She's such a sweet little girl. I sure hope her mama is going to be all right."

Oh, he certainly hoped the woman was right about that. "I need to drop this box in my car first." First. Was he really going to do this? Then again, what exactly was this?

"Of course. I'll be at the intake desk in the ER waiting room when you get back." The woman's smile didn't falter despite the seriousness of the situation.

Working his way across the parking lot, he hit the fob to open the trunk. Setting the box down, he stared at the contents again, as if perhaps that would explain to him what the heck was going on. *Katrina.*

Slamming the trunk of his Audi shut with one hand, he pulled out his phone with the other.

On the second ring, Katrina picked up. "How is she?"

"On her way to surgery."

"Serious?"

"I'm not sure, but she's not regained consciousness since the accident."

A deep intake of breath could be heard on the line.

"What I need for you to please see is who is her emergency contact on the HR forms, as well as any info on her daughter's father."

"The first I can find if you give me a minute, the second I don't think is in the scope of employee packet info."

If he was lucky, and he often was, maybe the emergency contact would be the child's father.

"Here we go." An uplifting tone gave him a moment of relief until her next words were nothing more than a grunt. "Hmm."

"What does hmm mean?"

"It means that you are her emergency contact."

"What?" That made no sense at all. He hadn't seen her in forever.

Things were going from baffling to completely crazy. What was it his grandfather always said; there's a fine line between insanity and genius, and Tess was pretty close to genius. Maybe she was just as close to insane. "Any info on the daughter?"

He could almost hear Katrina shaking her head. "Other than her age, twenty months, I didn't really expect to find anything on here. She does have Emma as the beneficiary for the company life insurance policy, but that's it."

"I see." Not that he did.

"What now?"

"Haven't a clue is probably not the right answer." There

was one thing he was sure of though; there was no way that Tess would want her little girl in the system even for a day. "How are you with toddlers?"

The deep cackle that exploded from his assistant was all the answer he needed. "Don't look at me. Only child and I didn't even baby-sit as a teen, but keep me posted."

"Will do." Looking up at the massive hospital complex, somewhere in there was a little girl and her only chance of staying out of the system was him. *Oh boy.*

"There you are." The same volunteer from earlier smiled up at Cooper. "Ready to get your girl?"

Why did all these people think he was Emma's father?

"Follow me."

With every step, he wondered what was he doing, why was he going along with the crowd. He could almost hear his mother's voice asking *If your friends jump off a bridge, are you going to follow?* These weren't friends, this wasn't a bridge, but apparently he did indeed intend to follow. At least for as long as it took him to figure out what was happening and come up with a better plan, because like it or not, he would not let Social Services have Emma. The problem was, what did he know of little girls? He had no business even considering taking charge of this child. And yet it was looking like that was exactly what he was going to do. Maybe he was the insane one?

"You don't have to worry." The volunteer looked away from the numbers lighting up overhead in the elevator and offered him what was no doubt intended to be a reassuring smile. "Emma isn't hurt. She's doing fine."

While he was worrying about the little girl, it was not for the reasons the volunteer thought.

Walking up to the desk on the pediatric floor, Sandy, the volunteer, stopped in front of a young blonde nurse standing at one end and cheerfully announced, "Emma's father is here."

The words 'Emma's father' couldn't have been more jarring if he really were her parent.

"Oh good." The blonde smiled up. "She's just a sweetie."

All he could do was nod. After all, what did he know about Tess' daughter?

"I'll leave him in your hands."

Sandy shook his hand before walking away, and the next thing he knew he was walking into a room with a cute little blonde kid sitting in a crib, sucking her thumb, and cradling a tiny blanket with a flamingo head.

The young girl stared at him with an intensity he hadn't expected from one so young. Then she looked at the nurse before lifting her arms in the air. "Up me down."

The nurse took a step back and frowning, Emma's gaze turned to Cooper.

For the life of him, he had no idea how to up down anyone, but logic told him that those arms up in the air meant she wanted out of the crib and obviously the nurse had no intention of doing it. Not for the first time, telling himself he was nuts, he reached out and lifted the child out of the crib, praying she didn't start screaming because some strange man had picked her up.

To his surprise, she didn't scream, didn't give him the stink eye, the child curled against him, her head tucked in his shoulder and her little fist gripping his shirt for dear life. If it were possible for a human heart to melt, his just did.

"Aw," the nurse sighed. "You'll need to sign some release papers. We have her diaper bag in the cabinet here."

Diapers? Oh boy. Again, what was he getting into? Looking up at the ceiling, he remembered his grandmother teaching him when a child hugs you, never let go first. The way little Emma was clutching him, he didn't think she was ever going to let go. "Where are the papers?"

"All ready at the floor desk."

He bobbed his head. "And where did you say the diaper bag is?"

The woman turned, opened a narrow cabinet and pulled out what looked to him to be an ordinary, if not colorful, backpack.

"We tried to get her to eat, but she wouldn't have any of it."

Add one more thing to the list of things he didn't have a clue about. Diapers, toddler food, and what the heck did he think he was doing?

At no point did Emma lift her head. Not when he grabbed the diaper bag, not when he signed the papers, and not when it dawned on him that he needed a car seat and pulled out his phone to call Katrina. So far she was one of the best assistants he could ask for. After a quick rundown of his dilemma, agreeing to meet him in the parking lot with a car seat as quickly as possible, he promised himself to give the woman a raise.

Standing by his car, waiting for his assistant, he considered his next move. Even if he wanted to buy everything Emma needed, what did he know about cribs and diapers and lord knew what else. What he needed was to take her home. To her home. "Forgive me, Tess." Popping the trunk, he hefted Emma a little higher, wondering how the heck women carried these kids around all the time. His left arm felt like it was going to fall off any minute now. With his right hand, he grabbed the purse and rummaged for Tess's wallet. He sure hoped her license had the correct address. Another minute and he found a few slips of paper, including the change of address receipt from her local post office. Good. At least he knew where she lived. He really hated searching through a woman's purse. His grandmother had always told him it was sacred territory. Finally, clipped deep inside, he found her keys. One of these should open the front door.

As he continued to make plans in his mind, a familiar red compact pulled up behind him. Out popped Katrina, and opening her back door, reappeared with a car seat in hand. "I bought the best recommended. My neighbor has a toddler and I remembered her saying these spinner seats are a God-send."

For a moment he wondered how her neighbor would feel about caring for one more kid. "Thanks." Considering he was an engineer and should be able to figure out how to place a baby in a car seat without much effort, he found himself reading every line of the directions before settling her in. He'd opted for the safer middle seat placement, and determined she was old enough to be forward facing, which meant he could see her in the rear-view mirror. Somehow that idea gave him a modicum of comfort. Not much, but a little of something was better than all of nothing.

Without a peep, Emma stared at him, then Katrina. Since she'd been so attached to the little blanket in the hospital room, he handed it to her along with a toy or two he'd found in the diaper bag and said another quick prayer that Tess would wake up quickly, recover even faster, and retrieve her daughter. Then she could explain why the heck he was her emergency contact.

"You going to be okay?" Katrina asked.

"I have no idea." He circled the car to the driver seat. "I don't suppose you want to—"

Without his saying another word, Katrina shook her head forcefully from side to side. "Not on your life. I have a hot date tonight. Surely you must know someone with children?"

The only person he knew was his cousin Mitch and their baby was much younger than Emma. "Maybe."

"Good. Then you're all set." She turned and waved. "I'm guessing I won't see you at work tomorrow."

Glancing at Emma tucked neatly into the back seat, he looked up at Katrina. "I honestly don't know." As a matter of fact, at the moment, he doubted there was anything he did know.

CHAPTER FOUR

Thanks to Houston traffic, the drive to Teresa's home took longer than Cooper would have liked, but at least Emma was quiet. That was a good thing. At least, he thought it was. Should she be talking and making noise? Maybe her silence was actually a bad sign? Or maybe he should have just let an experienced foster family take custody of the little girl until her mother was better.

Shaking his head, he looked up at the rear-view mirror. Of course that was not the better idea. The kid was staring ahead, sucking her thumb, and clutching that little blanket-like flamingo. Too small to actually be a blanket, he assumed it was a comfort thing. He also knew that clueless or not, taking custody of Emma had been the right thing to do. What he didn't know was what the heck to do next. If ever there was a time when Google was your friend, this was it. At the next red light, he took a moment to search the day of a toddler. A few more swipes and he found the perfect site to layout a typical schedule.

A horn honked behind him and he stepped on the gas. Never before had he wished for more red lights, but by the time he'd reached the quaint suburban house on a tree-lined street, he'd felt more confident about what he was supposed to do with the little girl. Starting with a nap. She needed a nap. And a snack. He prayed that finding those would be easy.

Pulling into the driveway, he parked in front of the detached garage and continuing his prayers with every step, managed to remove Emma from her seat without much fuss and even successfully unlocked the door with a toddler on his hip. Oddly enough, he was actually more proud of himself for accomplishing this small feat than he'd been with any other recent project in his life.

The home was bright and airy and clearly still in the process of being unpacked. Dropping the diaper bag on the sofa, he crossed the living room into the breakfast nook and on into the kitchen. Looking around, he spotted the pantry and started there. Bingo. Right in front of him was a shelf dedicated to what looked like kid snacks. At least he assumed that organic Nothing But Fruit oat bars and Goldfish crackers were her snacks. Another basket caught his eye. Fruit sauces in a pouch with a big red top. That did not look like something used for cooking. Lifting one, he paused to read the label, but Emma reached for it, trying to snatch it away.

"Would you like some apple sauce?"

Still no smile, but she did nod and softly, and clearly announced, "Yes."

Unscrewing the cap, he wondered, did he have to put her in a high chair, squeeze it into a bowl? Pausing again, the pouch in his one hand and Emma on his other hip, he studied the layout and opted to start checking the cabinets closest to the sink for dishes. He'd only taken a single step when Emma leaned forward and successfully snatched the pouch from his hand. At the same time he used his now free hand to help rebalance her on his hip, Emma shoved the pouch in her mouth and began sucking.

"Well, that was much easier than I thought." Now he had to wonder if the combination apple and banana sauce was enough or if he needed to offer her a bar or fish or something. As he glanced in the fridge and spotted similar pouches labeled yogurt, Emma shifted slightly in his arms and laid her head on his shoulder. "You must be tired."

After all, from what he'd read, children this age still need at least one nap a day. Circling around through what was supposed to be a formal dining room but looked more like a box warehouse, he continued back into the front hall and up the stairs. There was no missing Emma's room. If the one wall painted bubble gum pink wasn't a dead giveaway, the menagerie of stuffed animals and white crib removed any lingering doubt.

Letting the empty snack pouch fall to the floor and still clutching the flamingo blankie in her other arm, Emma flung herself toward the crib. Could it really be this easy?

Not knowing what else to do, he drew the curtains closed on the window—after all, he liked a dark room, so should a little kid—and then he set her inside the crib. Immediately, she reached for a pacifier that was in the corner, shoved it into her mouth and snuggled into the blankie. Had he ever seen anything so angelic in his life? "Sweet dreams, little one."

He almost wished he could just stand there and watch her sleep. How crazy was that? Slowly backing out of the room, he pulled the door closed and blew out a deep sigh. So far so good. But now what?

Why did her head hurt so much? Teresa tried to touch her temple, but her arm weighed more than a wet Persian cat. Why? Had she slept on it? So sleepy. *Emma.* Everything was so quiet. Emma must still be napping. Or was she still sleeping? Was it morning or afternoon? No. Had to be morning or why would she be in bed?

The way she struggled to open here eyes, it must be the middle of the night, but something didn't feel right. Maybe if she sat up. Okay, everything felt heavy, not just her arm. What the heck? Forcing one eye open, she tried desperately to focus. Her lids drifted shut again and one more time she tried to open her eyes and focus. The wall was white, not her wall. Wait, new house. Was this her new room?

Losing the battle of the eyelids, her eyes fluttered shut one more time. The banging in her head seemed more of a dull ache now.

"You need your rest. Everything will be okay."

Who said that? Was someone in the house? No. A dream. Was she dreaming? Everything was so very… fuzzy. Just five more minutes, then she'd get up and unpack. Yes. Five more minutes.

On the phone, doing his best to take care of some business while the little girl napped, Cooper churned his new responsibilities in the back of his mind, scribbling notes and doing internet searches between calls. The first thing he looked up was how long he could expect the baby to sleep. That response was all over the place. Apparently, he had between one and three hours. A couple of times he'd gone upstairs to listen at Emma's door but didn't hear a peep. Poor kid was probably exhausted.

The more he searched online the more keenly aware he was of just how little he knew about children. For one thing, apparently he was supposed to change her diaper before putting her down for a nap. Besides the few in the diaper bag, he didn't have a clue where more diapers were kept. For Emma's sake, he sure hoped the hospital had changed her before he came to see her.

Next, he perused the pantry and fridge, with little idea of what the heck he was supposed to feed her. He also didn't know when her bedtime was, or what was her bedtime routine. Nor did he know what time she would wake up in the morning or who was going to watch her the next day so he could go to work. Blowing out a deep sigh, he doubted he had ever felt so very useless. Or stupid.

Thinking things through, if he was going to stay here, he'd need to pack a bag. Then again, at first the idea of bringing the baby home to familiar surroundings sounded sensible, but now, he felt like he was invading Tess's privacy. Speaking of which. It struck him that surely by now she should be out of surgery, and hopefully someone would have more information for him.

All set to call the hospital, his phone dinged and at the same time, Emma let out a loud cry. Startled by it all, he sent the call to voice mail and turned away from the pantry, crossing the kitchen in two long strides. He simply could not do this alone. Not even with the advice of the internet. He had no idea how he was going to explain his being responsible for Emma, especially when he wasn't all that sure why himself, but this was most definitely a matter for someone wiser than him. As soon as he packed a bag and changed her diaper, Emma was coming with him to the ranch. The nursery for Mitch's daughter would work fine for Emma and his grandmother would know everything he didn't. Emma cried out again and heaving in a deep breath, he bolted up the stairs. Grams was definitely the answer.

Inching the door open, Emma sat gripping her flamingo blankie and sucking on her thumb. As soon as he entered the room, she pushed to her feet, extended her arms to him and lifting her up, was caught completely off guard when she once again snuggled into his shoulder. Was there anything sweeter in this world? "We're going to visit my grandmother. What do you think of that?"

"Yes," she muttered into his shoulder. For some reason he thought 'no' was the one word that all young children used. So far, Emma had been extremely agreeable. Opening the drapes, he patted her back with his free hand and scanned the room. The changing table was on the opposite wall and he suspected diapers and creams and anything else needed was probably in or near the piece of furniture.

Every time he tried to set her down, she clung even harder to him. He never would have guessed it possible, but apparently, he could pack a bag and carry a kid at the same time. He'd found an insulated bag in the pantry and filled it with the yogurts, the apple sauces and anything else that looked like it might be toddler food. With the bag in his car and Emma safely strapped into the car seat, he hopped into the car and backed out of the driveway. Just knowing he wasn't going to have to do this alone anymore was a massive relief. What he didn't understand was how did Tess do single parenthood? There wasn't a single sign of a man anywhere in the house. The only photos were of her and Emma.

From the car he called the house and told Margaret, the maid who'd been so much help when Gwyneth had Elizabeth, that he was coming with company. No point in explaining this over the phone, but at least he was assured both his grandparents were home and had no plans to go anywhere. He'd started to call the hospital when a truck cut him off and he swerved to avoid hitting the guardrail. Checking on Emma in the rear-view mirror, he decided definitely no more calls with a baby on board.

To his surprise, Emma was a good sport for the long drive out to the ranch. When he pulled into the driveway, her eyes seemed so full of curiosity as she took in every inch of her surroundings. Quickly, he retrieved her from the seat, kicked the car door shut with his foot, and hurried up the steps and inside. Knowing his grandparents would be in the parlor along with any other family members; he took a deep breath and patting Emma on the back, crossed the threshold into the large family room.

"Hello, dear." His grandmother concentrated on the crossword puzzle in front of her. "Margaret said you were…" her words trailed off as she lifted her head and spotted Cooper and company. "Oh, my. Who is this?" Immediately, Grams was on her feet and slowly moving toward him.

"Emma Gordon."

"Hello, Miss Emma."

The child tipped her head at Lila Baron, but didn't say a word. At least she didn't cry.

"If you could take her a minute, I'd like to call the hospital and check on her mother."

"Of course." The older woman, who looked a decade or two younger than her years, reached forward. To Cooper's relief, the child willingly went to his grandmother. If Emma was any judge of character, and he'd heard that children were excellent judges of character, she should know that Lila Baron was one of the good guys. The very good guys.

Turning and walking toward the window, and putting the phone on speaker, Cooper called the hospital. Whoever answered directed him to the appropriate nurse's station. It took a few rings, but someone finally picked up. "This is Cooper Baron. I'm calling in to see how Teresa Gordon is doing. I assume she's out of surgery?"

"Just a minute, Mr. Baron."

He had no idea what the person on the other end was doing, but waiting another few minutes for answers wasn't going to kill him. Especially since his grandmother and Emma were making fast friends over a game of pat-a-cake.

"Yes, Mr. Baron. I see here that you are Miss Gordon's emergency contact."

"Yes," he confirmed, not missing how his grandparents both raised their heads to glance at him.

"Oh, and it says here that Miss Gordon's daughter was released to her father's custody."

He bobbed his head and wished he hadn't put the dumb phone on speaker. One more thing he'd have to explain to the Governor and Grams. Especially since he didn't want to rectify the incorrect assumption if it meant Emma would be put in the foster-care system, even if only temporarily.

"And there are notes." The woman paused a moment. "I don't see a medical power of attorney on file, but since Emma's pediatrician is here at the hospital, we have access to her records and birth certificate listing you as the father. That's enough to allow us to update you."

Birth certificate? His brain was stuck on those few words muttered by the nurse. So much so, he ignored the way his grandmother's mouth fell open and his grandfather's brows pleated into a frown. There had to be a big mistake somewhere. There just had to be. He'd known a lot of people in his day, and yes, he and Tess had grown close his senior year, but just as good friends. He had most definitely never known Teresa Gordon in the biblical sense—ever.

CHAPTER FIVE

Blinking, Teresa squinted really tightly and then stared at an unfamiliar ceiling. Where the heck was she? A shuffling sound to her side had her blinking once more. Why was someone in her room?

"Welcome back." The sound came from a woman in pink standing beside her bed.

An effort to speak was halted by her tongue stuck to the roof of her mouth. Had she eaten a sock in her sleep?

"Hold on. Let's sit you up a bit and you can have some water." The woman pushed a button and Teresa's bed began lifting from behind.

This was nice. She didn't have the strength to move. Blinking again, as if that would somehow help clear the fog that filled her brain, she looked down at the sides of the bed. This was definitely not her bed and not her room.

"And here you go." The same lady held a tall plastic glass with a massive straw tilted in her direction.

Thankful the headache from earlier was gone; she closed her lips around the large straw and gulped the first few sips.

"Easy." The woman pulled the cup away. "How does that feel?"

Moving her lips, she managed to croak out, "Better."

Nodding her head, the woman returned the straw to her lips. "One more time, but slowly."

Doing as she was told, she swallowed a few more sips and let go of the straw. "Thank…you." Why was forming words so difficult?

"You are a very lucky woman."

The lady in pink—no wait, those were scrubs. A

doctor? Nurse? "Where am I?"

"You're at County Hospital."

Scanning the room again, she realized the woman was right. This was a hospital room. But how?

"You were in a wreck."

Wreck? "Emma!" Wanting to sit up, climb out of bed, and find her daughter was one thing, following through was apparently another as a tearing pain cut across her midsection.

"Whoa. Steady there or you'll rip out your stitches. You had surgery to stop the internal bleeding."

Bleeding? That couldn't be good. "Emma?"

"Emma is fine. And so are you. The doctor removed your spleen and all your numbers have come back good. I've seen much worse in your situation."

If she had to be in a category, she'd prefer not to be in the worse section. "Emma?" She had to know who had her daughter.

"She went home with her father."

Her eyes popped open and her brain started spinning. *Who*? *What*?

"Such a nice man. As soon as he picked her up, she hung on and didn't let go."

Nice man? What nice man? "I need—"

"You need to rest. If the next twenty-four hours go as well as the last few, they'll let you go home."

Home. That was better, but Emma. "Emma. I want to see her."

"The next time Mr. Baron calls to check on you, we'll let him know you're awake and asking for your daughter."

About to mutter thank you, the words registered more clearly in her head. Baron. Father. Holy…

The kid was fascinating. Cooper would pay big bucks to know what was going on in Emma's little mind. The way her gaze shifted from one person to the other whenever they spoke, he could almost see the wheels turning as she processed and made up her mind about who knew what. It was those intelligent eyes that had him and his grandparents putting off the upcoming conversation until after Emma was in bed.

"I didn't realize you owned a high chair." Emma was situated in a high chair with colorful plastic plates and toddler size flatware.

"We have everything needed for children." Grams smiled at him. He should have realized the moment news of a great-grandchild spread that his military grandfather and beloved grandmother would be ready for a passel of kids to make an appearance.

Emma had been placed beside him at the dinner table. Not sure when her bedtime or anything else was, the family opted to eat early, include Emma, and fortunately, she seemed to be on board with the plan. Though her fascination seemed to be with the two dogs lying on either side of her. Cooper actually had to shift his chair over a bit so that Honey could fit between him and the little girl. It was the first time he'd ever seen the dogs not at his grandparents' side.

"She's a good little eater." His grandmother smiled at the child.

Emma continued to watch everyone. A piece of macaroni and cheese stabbed at the end of her fork, she looked at the faces around the table before twisting the fork into her mouth.

"How come we didn't get mac and cheese?" Too tired to drive all the way home from a business expedition, Cooper's brother Devlin stopped at the ranch for dinner and a good night's sleep. It had been a while since he'd popped by. Too bad Cooper hadn't had his phone out when his brother arrived, because the look on Devlin's face when he spotted Emma had been beyond hilarious.

Hazel, the family cook, walked into the dining room, a grin on her face wider than Cooper had ever seen. "Here's your milk, little one."

Reaching for the sippy cup he'd brought from Tess's

home, Emma smiled up at Hazel. "Milk."

"Yes, sweetie."

It was the first time he'd seen her smile. The dimple on only one cheek reminded him so much of her mother. At first he'd been more than a little annoyed that his parents had hired a lowly freshman to tutor him, but once he got to know the sweet kid, he'd been impressed by her gumption and determination. Eventually, as Tess became more relaxed around him and smiled more often, the cute dimple on her cheek whenever she smiled even a little bit had become just one of the things about her that fascinated him.

Dinner progressed as if it had been any other night and he had not come home with a toddler in tow. Not a word was said about Emma or Tess or his conversation with the nurse. At one point he noticed Devlin's eyes rounding wide and when he turned to see the baby, her head was bobbing, her eyes were drooping and he was pretty sure any second now she was going to land in what little was left of her hot dogs and mac and cheese.

"Looks like someone is ready for bed." His grandmother looked straight at him. She didn't need to say anything for him to know it was time to put the little one to sleep.

"I guess that means me." He hoped for a volunteer. Especially in the diaper department.

"You are her father." Masked with a sweet forced smile, his grandmother's tone hovered between reproving and teasing.

"Her what?" Devlin's head snapped over to Cooper and back to Emma.

"It's not how it sounds."

"Really?" His brother stared at him. "Looks like I picked the perfect night to stop for an impromptu dinner."

"Remember to use the white paste on her bottom. It's going to be a long night." His grandmother was still smiling. "And close the blackout drapes in the nursery and you might as well turn on the sound machine. It might comfort her if she wakes up and realizes she's in a strange crib."

He bobbed his head and was very glad he'd brought the child here. He knew nothing about white paste, diapers, drapes, sound machines, or anything else to do with small children.

As she'd done every other time he'd picked her up, the moment Emma was out of the high chair and in his arms she snuggled into his shoulder. He had a feeling if he didn't hurry up; she'd be deep asleep long before he got a clean diaper and pajamas on her.

In the nursery, he spotted the small bookshelf beside a rocker and considered if he should read her a story, but then he decided maybe tomorrow. Tonight the sweet girl needed to go to sleep.

A few minutes later, he was downstairs rejoining the family at the dining room table.

"How did it go?" the Governor asked.

"Her diaper may be a little lopsided, but I think she'll be fine."

His grandmother smirked sweetly. "Now, do you want to explain to us why the hospital thinks you are Emma's father?"

Unfortunately, only one person could tell him why his name was on her daughter's birth certificate. According to the hospital, Tess had not only come out of surgery with flying colors, she'd already woken up a few times. The nurse had convinced him that she needed her rest and might not be very alert if he came by this evening, so he'd made up his mind to visit first thing in the morning.

"Well, brother?" Devlin stirred sugar into his coffee cup. "I'm rather curious myself."

"Trust me, big brother, you're not the only one."

CHAPTER SIX

All the grands had designated bedrooms at the ranch. Most were the same rooms they'd slept in as kids. Occasionally adults would be here at the same time and continue to share the room, but usually only a handful of Baron grandchildren were present at once. With so many marrying, a few bedrooms were redone into adult suites with queen or king size beds. In Cooper's case, he was delegated not to his usual room but to the room next to the nursery.

Most of the night he found himself rolling over and glancing at the clock, listening to see if he heard from Emma. No surprise that when he rolled over at 7 a.m. at the sound of the little girl talking to herself, he felt like he'd barely crawled into bed. He also found it fascinating listening to her babble. She seemed to be having a very animated conversation, but he could not decipher a single word. Remembering that his grandmother had mentioned a camera, he logged in on his phone and could see her sitting in bed, her flamingo blankie in her lap and clearly the recipient of all her thoughts.

Staring at the ceiling a moment, he considered his schedule for the day. So much to do. He'd start with having Katrina cancel anything that wasn't critical. Then he'd go to the hospital. Once he found out… a startling cry broke his train of thought. It actually took him a moment to register that it was Emma. Apparently, she'd grown tired of talking to herself. Grabbing his bathrobe, he shrugged into it and trotted across the room to the nursery. Easing the door open, he squinted to see inside.

It took a moment, but assisted by the light from his

room, creeping into hers, he spotted Emma standing in the crib, her arms up in the air. That he understood. What he hadn't been prepared for was the way she once again curled into his shoulder and rather than grab onto the fabric of his robe, her arms curled around him, she patted *his* arms.

Could she really be trying to comfort him? Did all toddlers do this? He'd figured out she was definitely a snuggler; then again, were all kids snugglers? Lord, he knew so little. How did real parents do it? There was little doubt in his mind that newborns did not come with manuals. Yes, every expert and his grandmother had written books, but it's not the same as direct from the manufacturer instructions.

"What do you say we get you out of your pajamas and dressed for breakfast?"

"Yes," her voice came out so low and sweet.

"Are you hungry?"

Her head lifted slightly, and her voice was stronger. "Yes."

"Okay, then." He was getting better at the diaper thing. The mini spatula like contraption that Gwyneth used for coating the baby's bottom made spreading the white cream way less messy, and he'd figured out balancing the tape evenly so her diaper wasn't so off kilter. Now that she was all dressed, all he had to figure out was how the heck was he supposed to shower and dress himself? Was it safe to leave her in the nursery alone? Was it okay to leave her in the bathroom with him? Good grief, if business decisions were this difficult, he'd be bankrupt. If ever there was a good reason to call in reinforcements, this was it.

Picking up the phone, he called the kitchen. Hazel answered and hiding her mirth as he spoke, agreed to come get Emma so he could dress. The hand-off was… interesting. Although, the little girl went easily to Hazel, Cooper was pretty sure she also gave him the stink eye for passing her off. Surely, he was imagining that, right? Shaking his head, he proceeded into the bathroom and must have broken a world record for showering and dressing and presenting himself for breakfast.

"She loves bacon." Grams glanced at him a moment before returning her smiling gaze to the little girl. "Her eyes remind me of your father."

He supposed that was better than saying they reminded her of him. "Green eyes are common." He took the seat beside Emma. "First thing on my agenda today is to visit Teresa."

"Always liked that girl." The Governor's gaze bore into him. "Smart and sweet. Reminds me of your grandmother."

About to cut into his French toast, Cooper casually glanced at each of his grandparents. The way the two kept watching Emma and smiling, he wasn't sure if they really didn't believe him or simply didn't want to. "Yes," he couldn't argue, "but we need to figure out what's going on and then I have to check out what's going on with the new hotel downtown."

"That's an ambitious day," his grandmother shifted her attention to him.

"No more than any other day." Even though visiting someone in the hospital wasn't typical for him, a full day and then some was.

"Yes, but any other day you're not toting a toddler around."

His fork stopped midway to his mouth. "What?"

Grams waved at the baby. "She's your responsibility."

"Well, yes, I suppose. But I thought…" his gaze drifted to the kitchen door. They had plenty of staff to lend a helping hand with Emma. The odds were pretty good that at least half of them, including Hazel, knew more about little girls than he did.

"You might want to think again." His grandfather stuck a finger out at Emma, and ducking his head, started making funny smiling faces.

Really? His grandfather, the former Marine and always tough guy, was making smiley faces at the toddler. His mind scrambling, he thought fast, suddenly extremely happy that Baron Enterprises had embraced on-site childcare for their employees a long time ago. Right about now, that should come in very handy. On the other hand, tongues would be wagging on the grapevine if he were the one to drop someone else's daughter off in daycare. Heaving a deep sigh, he came short of physically shaking his head. Now what?

There was little doubt in Teresa's mind that if she weren't on pain meds, she'd be in a world of hurt. Even with the meds flowing directly into her veins, she could still feel the discomfort in her side every time she moved. Whether it was to scratch her nose, or call the nurse, or reach for a mug of water, every little effort tugged at her side and reminded her that she had survived a car accident and subsequent surgery.

"You're looking better this morning." The same nurse who had woken her up what felt like every few minutes most of the night had the nerve to stand there smiling at her.

"You too."

The nurse chuckled. At least someone had a good sense of humor.

What Teresa needed wasn't compliments, she needed to get some answers—and fast. Who knew where Emma was, what kind of care she was getting. "My daughter. I need to get out of here and take care of my daughter."

"Your daughter is doing just fine," a low deep voice came from the doorway.

Blinking at the nurse messing with her IV and who knew what else, Teresa would have shaken her head if movement didn't make every muscle hurt. She had to be hearing things. None of the staff coming and going so far this morning had been a male.

"Wish I could say the same for you," the same voice came closer.

Shifting just enough to turn her head in the direction of the voice, foggy memories of someone telling her that Emma was with Cooper Baron came rushing forward. Until this very moment, she thought for sure that had been one of the many strange dreams she'd had. Unfortunately, the car accident was definitely not a dream, and apparently neither was Cooper Baron.

"How are you feeling?" Familiar deep green eyes, eyes that had sucked her in and threatened to scramble her brains more than once, smiled at her.

"Like I wrestled an eighteen-wheeler. And lost."

Cooper bobbed his head. "That's pretty much what happened, except the truck was only one ton with four wheels."

"Ugh," she groaned.

"Don't let her fool you." The nurse stepped away from the equipment and smiled at Cooper, then turned to Teresa. "Shift change is coming up. The doctor has already been by. Not sure if he'll be back later or not since you were sleeping, but everyone is very happy with your progress. Most people are not this alert."

"Good. Then I can go home."

The nurse shook her head. "Maybe in a few days. Usually after a surgery like yours, folks are in the hospital for at least a week, but if you keep this up, you'll be out of here sooner than later."

Sooner sounded good to her. "I need to get to my daughter." She would have liked to throw off the covers, jump to her feet, and prove to everyone that she was just fine. There was only one problem with that plan—she was far from fine.

"The best thing you can do for Emma is to take care of yourself." His expression an unreadable blank slate, Cooper now stood by her bed.

Oh how she hoped yesterday's conversation with the nurse telling her that her daughter's father, Cooper Baron, had taken Emma was just a foggy dream.

The nurse looked to Cooper. "You won't want to stay very long. I've given her something to help her sleep. She needs her rest."

Cooper nodded then waited for the nurse to leave and the room door to close behind her before he turned his attention back to Teresa.

"You know where she is?"

One eyebrow shot up and the single gesture told her loud and clear that the conversation she'd imagined had actually happened. "I do. We spent the night at the ranch. She's a sweet kid."

That made Teresa smile. "Is she asking for me?"

"Actually, no."

"Oh." She wasn't sure if she should be happy that Emma was okay, or disappointed that she didn't miss her. Obviously, happy was better, but still.

"She seems to just be taking everything in. Grams says that's the sign of a smart child. Like mother, like daughter."

"Thank you."

He shrugged. "It's just the truth. You were always very smart. Almost too smart. I won't be surprised if Emma's even smarter."

"No." She wished she could sit up more. "Thank you for taking care of her."

"I knew you wouldn't want her with Social Services."

"Social Services?" Every muscle in her sore body tensed.

Very gently, Cooper patted her arm. "Relax. They were never called in. Apparently, this hospital seems to be under the misconception that she's my daughter too."

"Oops."

"Oops?" His tone dropped. "That's it? Oops?"

She needed to explain, but suddenly, her eyelids were so heavy and her tongue felt so thick. Opening her mouth had become a monumental effort. Forming words seemed impossible, but she had to explain. Maybe…to-mor-row.

CHAPTER SEVEN

"What's the latest news on Teresa?" Katrina handed him a file.

"As far as I know the doctors are suggesting she might be able to go home tomorrow." The last few days had been a whirlwind from another dimension. Every morning he was up early enough to shower and dress before Emma woke up. Then he'd get her dressed and downstairs for breakfast. After that, he'd decided that avoiding daycare because of potential gossip was ridiculous, so he'd drive her to the daycare, do his best to get his work done without calling to check on her like he had the first two days until finally Sally the manager told him to relax and stay away.

For a split second he'd considered firing her for her bluntness, but quickly decided she was probably right. Real parents did not call daycare every hour to make sure their children were doing well. According to his grandmother, if Emma were disturbed by her surroundings and the changes in her routine, her disposition would show it. Since the child was usually smiling and playful, they could only assume all was well.

"You're fading again." Katrina waved a hand in front of him.

This wouldn't be the first time he'd been unable to concentrate on business. He'd gone to the hospital in person to see Tess again, but each time, she'd been sound asleep. They'd spoken on the phone a few times, but mostly just sharing health updates and reports on Emma. He still had no idea how his name was on Emma's birth certificate, though he did double check to confirm that was indeed the case. At first he was obviously confused. Who does that? Then he shifted quickly to downright furious. If it was money she was after why didn't she just come to him? Or was this some long-term plan for Emma to one day stake a claim to the Baron fortune? Not that it would work. There was no doubt he was not the child's father; no DNA test would prove otherwise. So what was the motive? The more he considered the possibilities, and thought back on the young woman who had helped him pass physics and get accepted to A&M, who had laughed and joked with him and his family, he couldn't believe anything bad about her.

Whatever her reason was, over the phone wasn't the time to find answers. Especially since, even though Tess sounded stronger, she was still weak. He could hear the frailty in her voice and the struggle to hide it. At the sound of her soft voice asking for her daughter, inquiring over every detail of her day, his anger would soften and then he'd remember Tess's smile, how excited she was for him when he passed his last physics test, how she'd shiver when she ate her ice cream too fast, there wasn't a devious bone in her body. There just had to be a good reason.

"And there you go again. Maybe I'll just go back to my desk and check my email." Katrina chuckled and took a step back.

"Sorry."

She shook her head at him. "I know it can't be easy to be surprised one day with the responsibility of a toddler, but at least her mother will be home soon. Who's going to help her?"

"What?"

"You know how much work a toddler is. Most people fresh out of the hospital need some time to finish recuperating. She is going to have help, isn't she?"

According to the nurse who had told him that she might be released soon, the woman had said something about three or four weeks to full recovery, but he hadn't considered what exactly that meant. "Good question."

"One that maybe you should find the answer to? After all, Emma's care is your first responsibility."

He nodded. Though he had no idea, why or how it happened, but he definitely agreed with his assistant. Emma's care was very much his responsibility, and making sure that her mother got the care she needed to take over the job once again was about to become his responsibility as well.

"It's official." The same nurse who Teresa had found so annoying just a few days ago, was grinning at her like the Cheshire Cat.

"What is?"

"You're going home today. Doc Morgan signed off on it a short while ago."

Home. Thank heaven. She was growing weary of lying in bed all day. She had a daughter to raise and a new job to start and a long list of things she wanted to accomplish for both. Although, she had no idea how, when moving around wasn't all that easy. "Not that I'm complaining, but didn't he say I'd be here a full week at least?"

"He did. That's pretty normal." The nurse erased her name from the board as she would be going off duty shortly. "But you're doing much better. There's nothing we can do for you here that you can't do at home."

Right now, she couldn't picture doing anything alone at home. Her mind began rushing through all the things she'd need once she got home with Emma. Help kept jumping to the top of the list.

Closing her eyes, she sucked in several deep breaths. She was a project manager. All she had to do was organize and manage; she could probably do that from home. Maybe. But, winning the lottery wouldn't hurt. She'd used most of her signing bonus for the first months rent and deposit as well as picking up a few pieces of furniture for the much bigger home. If she could find someone to help her around the house, she might be able to afford them for a couple of weeks. Surely by then she'd be able to take care of Emma by herself. She'd also have to deal with replacing her car, but that would have to wait. "How long before I can leave?"

"As soon as someone comes for you and we can give them your care instructions."

Well, that might be a problem. If she spoke out loud that there was no one, did that mean she'd have to stay longer? Continue to rely on Cooper's kindness for Emma's care? Did she have a choice? Maybe with one more day. She needed a little time to research and plan. Which meant she needed internet connection. Her laptop preferably, but a tablet would do. A small hammer began banging against her temple.

"Hello," Cooper greeted the shift nurse.

"I thought you'd be the one coming for Miss Gordon."

Teresa looked from the nurse to Cooper, her mind struggling to put the pieces together. The doctor might think she was improving quickly, but her scrambled brain said otherwise. Normally she was always three steps ahead of everyone in the room. A quick survey of the situation and she'd formulate a detailed plan within minutes. Thinking that fast drove some of her coworkers crazy at her last job. Right now, she couldn't plan her way to the bathroom.

"I thought you'd be dressed and ready to go. Or am I too early?"

"I just heard that I'm being released today." It was a lame response, but the truth.

Cooper nodded. "I wasn't far. When I called for an update and one of the nurses told me that she was expecting the papers to be signed for your release today, I went ahead and came over. Thought we needed to talk anyhow."

Oh boy, did they need to talk. He probably hated her. Though he hid it well.

"Oh." Cooper snapped his fingers. "When I passed the desk, a nurse asked me to tell you that she'd be in shortly to give you the care instructions."

"Yes, about that. I'm going to have to do some fast work to get everything in place at my house."

Shaking his head, Cooper took a step closer to her bed. "Grams insists you come to the ranch. The nurse explained you still have a few weeks of recovery time."

"The ranch?" She couldn't impose on these good people any more. Though it was nice to know she'd at least been right about one thing when it came to the Barons and Emma.

"Don't bother arguing. Grams may be a lot of years older than the last time you saw her, but she hasn't changed one lick."

Memories of the gentle matriarch flooded her mind. Once the Governor had said his wife reminded him of a velvet hammer. Soft, beautiful, unique and deadly when swinging. As far as she could remember, Lila Baron always got her way. "I don't know."

"If she lives alone, can she still go home?" Cooper looked to the nurse.

The woman didn't say a word; she merely shrugged and shook her head.

"That's what I thought." Cooper blew out a soft sigh and seemed to struggle to smile. "Looks to me like you have two choices: the ranch or staying put."

Not much of a choice if you asked her. "Where's Emma?"

Now his smile bloomed in earnest. "When I learned I'd be detouring to pick you up, I swapped cars with Devlin. He took her to the ranch for me."

"Devlin?"

Cooper chuckled. "Don't look so surprised. That little one has the whole family wrapped around her cute little finger."

Already exhausted from holding her own head up, Teresa leaned back. Resisting the urge to close her eyes and take a nap, she caught the way Cooper's eyes narrowed as he watched her.

The nurse paused at the foot of Teresa's bed. "I'm going to see what's taking those instructions so long. When I come back, I'll help you get dressed."

"Oh, right." Did she even have any clothes?

As if reading her mind, Cooper lifted a plain shopping bag. "I was told you'd be more comfortable in oversized t-shirts for now. I hope you don't mind Fruit of the Loom."

T-shirts? Oh, boy. Could things get any more embarrassing?

CHAPTER EIGHT

This entire situation was beyond surreal. Not even considering that for almost a week Cooper had been responsible for a toddler—granted with a bit of help, but still—he'd been playing daddy and even more startling, enjoying it. Ignoring the fact that for some still unknown reason everyone, including his grandparents despite his reassurances to the contrary, seemed to believe he was Emma's biological father. Regardless of those completely out of the ordinary and borderline unbelievable scenarios, what he seemed to struggle with most right now, was that Teresa Gordon, after all these years, was seated beside him.

If he ignored the circumstances, he could almost make himself believe he'd traveled back in time. Back to high school, back to stressing out about his grades, to struggling to stay awake and alert, and to forcing his Baron-sized ego to accept that he needed the then fourteen-year-old freshman brainiac to save his GPA and his dreams of A&M. And back to the young girl who, no matter what, could always make him smile. Only now, she wasn't fourteen, she was all grown up, and even weak and worn out, lit up the room.

At first, he'd thought the drive to the ranch would be the perfect time to talk and find out what had she been thinking. What was her intention? Once he'd settled Tess into the passenger seat, by the time he'd reached the driver side, she was sound asleep. They were only a few minutes out from the ranch and she hadn't even blinked. Sleeping so soundly, her exhaustion made him wonder if the hospital had released her too soon. Thank heavens she wasn't going home alone but to the ranch. He had a feeling there would be quite a bit of convalescence involved in the next few weeks.

Coming to a full stop in front of the house, he debated what to do now. Obviously, he needed to wake her up. On the other hand, perhaps letting her sleep wasn't a bad thing. But in the car? A tap on his window startled him. Looking over his shoulder, Devlin stood on the other side of the glass, frowning.

Hitting the button to lower the window, he whispered at his brother. "What?"

"Emma is in a mood. I think seeing her mom might help, but not if you two sit out here parked like a couple of teens on Lovers Lane."

Wasn't that a laugh? Aside from not having seen Tess in more years than he cared to count, and even though he'd always regretted losing touch after she'd left for college, the poor woman couldn't hold her eyes open, hardly apropos for a visit to Lovers Lane. "I hate to wake her up."

Devlin glanced around him and sighed. "Well, you can't leave her out here in the car."

No, he knew that. Opening the door, and nudging his brother back, Cooper climbed out of the car and circled around to Tess's side. Slowly opening the door, he squatted beside her. "Hey, sleepy head."

She didn't budge.

Gently tapping her knee, he tried again. "Tess. We're home."

Her head moved and she struggled to open her eyes.

"I'd better go back inside and have Grams distract Emma. I have a feeling that it would be better for Emma to see her mom more fully awake."

"Agreed." Right now he was actually very concerned how Emma might react to her groggy and weak mother. Not that long ago he would have assumed what an almost two year old would know about adult behavior. Only a few days with Emma and he was pretty sure there wasn't a single thing that kid missed. Most definitely, she would notice the changes in her mother and he did not want the child frightened. "Tess."

She blinked again, and then squinted at the sun hanging low in the sky. "Where am I?"

"Paradise Ridge."

Confusion settled into deep lines on her forehead.

"The ranch. You've been here before." This was not going the way he expected.

Still frowning, she looked around him at the front door. The moment a slow smile teased at the corners of her mouth, he knew she realized where she was. Oddly, it made him feel good that the revelation brought a smile to her face.

"Let's get inside and see Emma."

"Emma." Her smile brightened even more and her head lolled back onto the headrest.

"Okay, sleepy head. Come on." Having given up on waking her up without a large pot of coffee, he slipped his arm under her knees and the other around her back. In another moment, she was curled against him as he climbed the front steps. "Here we go."

The front door opened. "Welcome home, Mr. Cooper."

"Thanks, Jeeves."

"Yes, sir. Your grandparents are expecting you in the parlor."

He bobbed his head and marched into the front parlor. Without saying a word, his grandmother pointed to one of his favorite chairs. Another minute and Tess was settled comfortably, and more importantly, waking up.

"Thought you might like a little refreshment." Hazel smiled at their latest houseguest and set a glass of her fresh squeezed lemonade on the side table. Taking a step back, her gaze met Cooper's and he could read the concern in her eyes as easily as he could have had she written it on a piece of paper.

Offering a grateful smile, Tess reached for the glass and took a long slow sip. "Oh, that is good. I thought that my memories of Hazel's lemonade had been built up more than the reality." Holding the glass in front of her, she shook her head. "It's even better than I remembered."

Not sure what else to do for her, Cooper grabbed a fleece blanket out of a nearby basket and stretched it out over Tess's lap.

"I don't need a blanket." Tess took another sip. She seemed to finally be waking up. "Where is Emma?"

Still holding the unfolded blanket out in front of her, Cooper looked to his grandmother.

"Margaret has her in the kitchen eating a snack. She's especially fond of yogurt and Goldfish."

Tess smiled. "She'd live on it if I let her." Lips pressed tightly together, no doubt in an effort to hide her discomfort, Tess set the glass down on the table, waved Cooper and his blanket away, and easing herself back against the chair, smiled up at him. "When can I see my baby?"

From the moment Teresa had woken in the hospital and was fully aware of what was going on, all she could think about was holding her little girl. The current situation, the accident leaving her incapable of caring for her own daughter, confirmed that the Barons were still a family she could count on. What she wasn't sure of was how much they knew about the father mix up and if anyone would be angry with her when they found out.

"Look who's here."

Nothing made Tess's heart sing like Emma's smile.

"Mama." Her pudgy little arms stretched out, she leaned toward her.

"Whoa, sweetie," Cooper chuckled softly, his grip on the little girl tightening as he handed Emma off to her mother. "Careful. Mommy has an owy."

"Owy." Frowning, Emma cocked her head at her mother.

The interaction between this bachelor and her little girl had so much emotion surging in Teresa's chest, she didn't know if she should smile, cry, or get down on her knees and thank heaven for bringing this man back into her life, even if only as a friend.

Pulling her daughter against her chest, Teresa squeezed as hard as she could without hurting herself or Emma. "Who's Mama's favorite girl?"

Emma wrapped her little arms around her mother, then leaned back and grinning widely, shouted, "Emma!"

"Yes, Emma is Mama's favorite girl. And who is Mama's big girl?"

"Emma!" she patted her hands on Teresa's chest. "Emma a big girl."

"Yes, you are." She curled her arms around her daughter again and just breathed in the sweet scent of toddler and enjoyed how her soft locks of hair tickled Teresa's cheek. "I love you."

"Wuv you," Emma repeated and leaned back, sitting on Teresa's lap, leaving several inches of space between them.

Taking her daughter's cue, Teresa pointed at herself, "I," then made an X with her arms across her chest, "love," And using her pointer finger directed at Emma lilted, "you."

"Mama," Emma whispered gleefully.

Aware suddenly how intently the people in the room were watching her, she cleared her throat. "It's a game we've played since she first started learning words."

Mrs. Baron nodded. "We noticed she uses some sign language, but didn't see any signs of hearing loss."

"No," Teresa shook her head, "she learned it from a favorite TV show."

"I see." Lila Baron nodded, her focus, and smile, on Emma.

For the next few minutes they played pat-a-cake, and sang the itsy-bitsy spider with Emma trying desperately to mimic her mother's finger movements, and then Emma crawled down from her mother's lap, did her waddled run across the room to where a dog sat at Mrs. Baron's feet. Emma plopped down on the floor and throwing herself on the animal, wrapped her arms around the pup and rubbing her face in the fur, gleefully announced, "Doggy."

Teresa chuckled, then pressed her hand around her middle to stop the pulling pain.

"Easy there." Cooper stood halfway between her and

Emma, as if he were a sheep dog trying to view all of his flock, ready to pounce at the first sign of danger.

To Teresa's surprise, the dog barely budged until Emma sat upright and the dog rolled over on its back.

"Gentle," Cooper encouraged as Emma stretched out her hand and rubbed the dog's under belly. "Atta girl. Nice and easy."

"Mama," Emma shouted happily to her mother, "doggy!"

"Yes, sweetie. A very nice doggy."

"Mama," Emma repeated.

"I'm right here."

"Doggy." She tried this time and it finally struck Teresa that her daughter wanted her to go pet the doggy.

"Mommy will visit with the doggy later."

"Mommy needs to rest her owy," Cooper offered.

Emma frowned again, obviously debating something about her mother's owy, and finally toddled back. "Up me down."

"Climb on up." Teresa knew full well lifting her daughter onto her lap would not be a good idea.

"Up me down," her baby's tone grew stronger.

"Let me help." Cooper swept her up off the floor, spun her about once while making zoom noises, and then set Emma down on Teresa's lap. "And a perfect landing!"

Emma clapped, Cooper clapped, every Baron in the room clapped. Just one big happy family. Except no matter what she put down on any piece of paper, and no matter how gracious they all were, they still weren't her family.

CHAPTER NINE

"Time for bed." The entire family had taken to eating dinner early so that Emma could join them and then be put to bed before dessert. So far it had been working well, but tonight, Cooper didn't know what to expect.

Emma lifted her gaze to meet Cooper's, then looked to her other side. "Mama."

"Yes, baby." Tess smiled at her child.

"Mama."

If he were to venture a guess, Cooper would bet money Emma's clear enunciation of her mother's name was not an announcement but a declaration. She wanted her mother to put her to bed. "Come on, little one." The same as he'd done every night since her arrival, Cooper removed her dinner plates from the table, wiped her hands and mouth clean with the warm washcloth Hazel had left folded at her side, and then lifting the chair tray, unsnapped the safety buckle.

"Mama." Leaning over, Emma snatched hold of Tess's finger.

Tess lifted her gaze to meet his. A silent question of *now what* seemed to be crossing both their minds. At that moment, Emma's lower lip quivered and panic slowly crawled up his spine.

Thank heaven for Grams. In a second, she was on her feet and taking Emma into her arms. "Let's go upstairs, and your mommy will follow."

Even though her lower lip stopped puckering, Emma didn't seem convinced until her mother slowly rose from the chair. Understanding Grams could be trusted, the blonde cherub rested her head on his grandmother's shoulder.

"Help her up the stairs," his grandmother directed as she left the room.

There had been no need for the directive, he had no intention of letting Tess struggle on her own. Extending a hand to Tess, he added what he hoped was a reassuring smile.

She sucked in a deep breath and shoved to her feet. "Thanks, but I got this." Walking very slowly, almost shuffling, she seemed to be running low on fuel.

He had his doubts she would make it across the foyer, never mind up the stairs. As a matter of fact, now that he thought about it, if driving was out of the question for at least ten days, where did stairs fall into the restrictions?

The moment they reached the bottom of the stairs, Tess lifted her gaze to Grams and Emma already at the top and starting down the hall.

"Allow me." Without waiting for her response, he gently wrapped one arm around her waist and then scooped her up off the floor with the other.

A loud gasped escaped her throat, as her arms flew around his neck, and her mouth fell open. "What are you doing?"

"What does it look like I'm doing?" He took the first step and her hold on him tightened.

"You can't carry me all the way up those stairs."

"Watch me." Whether that was an overestimate of her weight, an underestimate of his strength, or a potshot at his manhood, he didn't know or care. Climbing the stairs on her own steam was simply not a good idea.

"I can walk on my own."

"I'm sure you can. But if the doctor doesn't want you driving, I doubt he wants you climbing up this massive staircase."

Her lips pressed tightly into a thin line, and she huffed out a deep breath, not very different from a snorting bull, but at least he'd won the argument.

Stepping onto the landing, she loosened her hold on him. "You can put me down now."

He shook his head. "Not till we get to Emma's room."

"She has her own room?"

"Sort of." He shrugged. "It's the nursery for my cousin Mitch's little girl. The first great-grandchild in the family. Most likely with hopes of many more." To one side of the open doorway, he set her down so that Emma would not see him carrying her.

"Thank you." She blew out another heavy breath. "You were probably right. I'm tired already and you did all the work."

That was the sense of humor he remembered from all those years ago. He didn't see it often, but when she let her lighter side show, it always made him smile. "You're welcome."

In the room, his grandmother already had Emma washed up and in her pajamas. "There's your mommy."

Her head turned, Emma grinned widely at the sight of her mother.

"Why don't you have a seat in the rocker, and I'll put Emma in your lap," Grams wisely suggested, already aware that Tess was not allowed to carry more than ten pounds.

Another minute and Tess was reading to Emma curled against her. He suspected strongly that Tess was enjoying this time as much as Emma. He'd already learned that reading to the sweet little girl just before bed was something he looked forward to, of course her mother had to enjoy it as well. He also suspected that tonight, Tess might take a little longer and read a little more to make up for lost time together.

Even though he hadn't known what to expect, deep down he had feared that a small fit of some kind might have ensued with her mother here but with limited mobility. Considering Emma had yet to throw a true crying fit, he really shouldn't have worried. As her eyelids grew droopy, her mother closed the book and nodded at him. Quietly over her down soft hair, he whispered a short good night prayer as he carried her to the crib. Another few minutes and she was snuggled in with her pacifier, her stuffed lamb and sound asleep.

"I've always thought this is what angels must look like." Tess stood over her crib taking in the sleeping child.

"Can't argue with that." He rested his hand along the small of her back. "Do you want to return downstairs for dessert, or is it your bedtime too?"

"Actually, it's been a long time since I've had any of Hazel's apple pie. Do you think I could have a slice in bed?"

He chuckled. Crawling into bed with a good book and a slice of any of Hazel's pies was always a good idea. "I bet something could be arranged."

"Good. Where am I sleeping?"

"This way." He gestured to the next-door over. "I'm sleeping in the adjoining room, and you'll be on the other side of Emma. Close enough if she needs you."

They'd barely made it into the hall when Margaret came onto the landing carrying a tray. "Miss Lila said that Miss Teresa should get some rest now also, but Hazel sent me up with pie and her special bedtime tea."

"Excellent. Thank you, Margaret." Cooper opened the bedroom door and gestured for Tess to go inside, then turned to Margaret. "Leave the tray on the dresser. I'll see to it that she's settled in."

Margaret nodded. "Hazel sent up two cups and two slices of pie."

"Thank you, Margaret."

The woman quickly exited the room. Cooper turned to see Tess staring at her bed. A very high bed.

"Let me." He went to lift her up the same as he had with the stairs.

"Do you have any idea how ridiculous I feel having you carry me everywhere?"

He shrugged. "Probably not, but you can't climb up there on your own. Tomorrow, we'll have Jeeves remove the box spring and place a board underneath for support instead. Then you should be able to sit more easily on the mattress."

"Thank you."

"You're welcome. And once you're tucked in, maybe

over Hazel's pie and tea, you can tell me about Emma's real father."

The conversation had to happen, Teresa knew that. Her palms sweating, she wiped them on her shirt. She'd never liked the unknown. She was a planner and there were too many unknowns in this conversation she was definitely not looking forward to. Especially since most of it didn't make sense even to her. It didn't help the situation at all that Cooper was being so kind and so ridiculously patient with her. Then again, those were some of the endearing qualities that she remembered about him all these years.

In the short while since he'd set her down on the bed, he'd gathered pillows to support her back, tucked her in under the covers as if she were a two-year-old like Emma, set her tea cup on the nightstand and handed her the plate with the warmed slice of pie.

Sitting across from her now, he lifted his fork in the air as though making a toast. "Bon appetite."

She dug into the pie and actually sighed. "So good."

One corner of his mouth lifted in a lazy smile. "No one makes pie like Hazel." Setting his dish down on his lap, he tipped his head to one side. "Where shall we start?"

Sucking in a fortifying breath, she blew it out very slowly. "Do you remember the day you got your final grade for physics?"

"Absolutely, the only time in my life that I cheered for a C-plus. All I needed was a C to keep my GPA where it needed to be."

"Your friends were cheering and rallying and everyone wanted to go celebrate."

"We did too."

"But not until after you took me to dinner."

His smile tipped up again. "I owed you."

"No. I owed you. If you hadn't believed in me as much as I believed in you, I would never have gotten the Baron

Scholarship when I graduated."

"You didn't need me for that. You were, and probably still are, the smartest woman I know."

"Thank you for that, but I think there are probably a few women in your life, starting with your own sisters, who would disagree." She lifted her hand to stop him from arguing. "But I digress. One of the things I've never forgotten was how you humored me."

His smile slipped and his brows buckled in confusion. "Humored you?"

"Over dessert." She waved her fork over her plate. "Not as good as this, but we had pie and laughed and joked and I told you if neither of us was married by the time I turned thirty, I'd come looking for you."

From the way he chuckled, she figured he remembered. "That's right. And I agreed. Mostly because I knew there'd be more than one man falling all over themselves to win you over by then, but partly," his smile softened, "because I knew if that ever happened, I'd be getting the better end of the deal." His head tilted to one side. "You must have been around thirty when you had Emma."

"Thirty-one."

"But you never married." It wasn't a question. He knew her records. "What happened to Emma's father?"

"Nothing that I know of."

His brows buckled and his gaze narrowed and his eyes turned cold. Not till his one fist clenched at his side did she realize where his mind must have gone.

"No. Nothing like that. Emma's biological father is a frozen pop."

"A what?" The utter confusion on his face reminded her of those first weeks trying to wrap his head around physics.

"I picked him out of a catalogue. Tall, blonde, green eyes, grad student, high IQ, no negative medical history. Just a number on a list."

"Why would you do that?"

She shrugged. "I was never very good at making friends."

"Of course you were. We were friends."

They were. He didn't know it, but he'd become her best friend by the time he graduated. And she'd been proud that they'd kept in touch from time to time. He'd even been kind enough to escort her to her senior prom. That was the night that the Baron family broke the news about the scholarship they'd created for her and other foster kids. "One friend. I hung out with a few girls at school from time to time, but no one came to my house and no one invites the foster kid to theirs."

His frown deepened. "But you weren't a foster kid in college. Surely you made friends there?"

"A few. But I was focused on school. Graduated in three years. Then I threw myself into my work. One day I looked up and I was thirty with no close friends, no man in sight. I tried the dating apps a few times and didn't see that making any difference. My biological clock won. I had to do something if I wanted a family of my own and a frozen pop made more sense than a silly teenagers bargain."

"We did pinky swear," he teased.

She'd always loved how he'd find a way to make her smile when her serious side kept her uber stressed. Like now. "We did, but I don't think you'd be smiling if I'd actually come by to collect."

"Okay, so none of this explains how I wound up on Emma's birth certificate."

"It does if you'd been in labor for thirty-two hours."

He sucked in a wince. "Having been here waiting when Gwyneth had her little girl, I have a better understanding of just how long that is."

"Very long. I wound up with an emergency C-section— and a lot of drugs. I had an allergic reaction to something they gave me and they had a hard time waking me up at all. Somewhere my fogged brain had me slipping in and out of reality. When I gave them the baby's name for the birth certificate, they asked me for my name, which I thankfully remembered. Though I may have first told them Princess Tess—"

"I didn't think you liked it when I called you that."

Not then and not now would she confess that she'd

loved the silly nickname; instead she merely shrugged. "Fortunately, they knew better than to write that down and had me repeat my full name. Next they asked me the baby's name. I'd actually planned to name her Emily, but in my loopiness, I'd said Emma, so Emma she is. And actually, I like it better anyhow."

"I suppose that's a good thing."

"Emma Elizabeth. I liked the idea of double initials." Carefully, she set her empty plate on the nightstand beside the tea cup. "And I apparently must have been dreaming of our little deal, because not only did I refer to myself by your nickname for me, when they asked for the father's name, I gave them yours."

"I see." His chin dipped, and he leaned back in the arm chair. "And it didn't occur to you to correct that once your brain was no longer in a fog?"

Heaving a sigh, she nodded. "Honestly, I didn't remember what had happened until recently when I had to get a copy of her birth certificate for my insurance with Baron Enterprises. It was a bit of a shock when I connected the dots. But it also occurred to me that if anything were to happen to me, there was no one to take care of Emma. No one to keep her out of the foster care system, and deep down I knew, the way your family was so kind to me in school, and then created that scholarship and made sure that I had everything I needed in college, I just knew that no matter why, you and your family would take care of her." Waving her hands in an upward gesture, she shrugged one shoulder. "The discovery got me thinking that I need a real plan for Emma if anything happens to me."

He nodded.

"Knowing I was moving back to Texas, I considered asking you to be her guardian."

"Me?"

She shrugged. "You were the closest friend I had, and the nicest person I know. But I thought it might go over better if I waited until after we'd settled in, and you'd had some time to get to know Emma—after all, no one expects to actually die young."

Except for a slight shake of his head, he remained perfectly quiet and still.

"For what it's worth, though I didn't die in that accident, I now know I was right about at least one thing. Sight unseen, you stepped up to the plate for my baby girl."

There, she'd said her piece and no one was ranting or raving or threatening to fire her or throw her and her daughter out on the curb. So far.

CHAPTER TEN

The same as the days before Tess's arrival, Cooper could hear Emma talking to herself in bed. Now, showered, dressed and sipping on his first cup of coffee while staring at his phone, he could see her sitting up, holding the rag doll he'd picked up for her after work the other day, and explaining something he did not understand in great detail. The interaction made him smile.

All night, he'd either tossed and turned, or had snatches of restless dreams. There was a vague memory of one dream that had him back in high school with Tess tutoring him in home economics and the fine art of pie baking, followed by diaper changing. No doubt all stemming from last night's conversation before Tess dozed off after finishing her pie. At least he'd heard the whole story before she faded off.

What he couldn't decide was how to react to the whole thing. After all, what's done is done. His name was on the birth certificate and that had allowed Emma to be placed in his custody. The possibility of her having wound up in one of the many subpar foster homes if he had not been on the certificate, or official guardian, made his skin crawl. Tess was right about one thing—every parent, single or not, should have a plan in place for their child's care if something should happen to them. What he wasn't convinced of was if he would be the best choice. He was, however, sure that his name needed to be removed from the birth certificate. As much as he would love to have a precious sweet child like Emma in his life some day, his name had no business being on her birth certificate.

A glance at his phone and Emma was now on her feet

rocking the crib. For a moment he wondered how long before she learned how to climb out of the thing. At what age was that normal? Not that it mattered. Time to get the buttercup.

Just as he pulled the door open, he was stopped by Tess standing, arm in the air ready to knock. "Sorry. It's time to get Emma and I'm afraid if I go in there alone she's going to expect me to pick her up."

"You mean up me down?" He got such a kick out of that toddler oxymoron.

Tess smiled at him. "Yeah. I'm going to hate it when she finally starts defining pick-me-up or put-me-down."

He knew exactly what she meant.

"Also…" she nibbled on her lower lip.

Instantly, he was transported to a table in the school library all those years ago. Only this time, besides finding her nervous gesture cute, his gut clenched and his pulse kicked up a few beats. What the heck?

Her gaze dropped to her robe. "I don't own any loose cotton clothes without waist bands or belts. I'm going to need to do a little shopping."

"Didn't like the t-shirts I bought you?" He bit back a smile.

"This one is super comfy and nice and long," she chuckled softly, "but it looks like I'm wearing your clothes, not mine, and I don't want to wear a robe all day long either. I'd like to try and update myself on what's going on at the office, at least a little. If I wind up on a Zoom call, I'm not going to look very professional in men's t-shirts."

She did have a point. He bought the softest cotton he could find in a big and tall size, but they were definitely not a fashion statement. And nothing close to business attire, though he'd prefer she recovered a little more before dealing with her job.

"I could call a car, but I wondered if maybe I could use your driver."

He shook his head. "No need. I'll take you."

"Are you sure you have time?"

"Absolutely." Katrina was going to kill him when he

told her he was taking the morning off, or maybe the whole day. "Now, shall we get your daughter?"

Emma must have heard them talking outside the door, because she stood facing them when they entered the room. That sweet smile could brighten the darkest of days. The kid seemed to have a better handle on the new routine than they did. Whenever he and Tess bumped into each other, Emma simply waited patiently for them to reposition. When changing her diaper or putting on her clothes, she raised a leg or arm to help, but when she was all dressed, she turned to Cooper asserting *up me down*, quickly having figured out they weren't letting her mother carry her.

Breakfast had gone the same as every other morning. The kid had a hollow leg and a definite love of bacon and Hazel's pancakes. Rather than drop her off at the office daycare, it was decided that Emma would stay with Grams and the staff. He had his doubts if she was going to get her nap with all the attention.

"Ready?" Cooper knocked on Tess's bedroom door.

"Coming." Once the door opened, Tess stood in a blue beach coverup that he didn't recognize.

"I didn't buy that?"

She shook her head. "It's your grandmother's."

"That belongs to my grandmother?" The sleeveless v-neck t-shirt dress in slate blue with a few star fish and bubbles along the hemline didn't fit his image of his grandmother.

"I think she said she bought it for Siobhan and then forgot about it."

That made more sense.

"It's not high fashion, but it does look a little better for going out in public."

Actually, as far as he was concerned, the woman could wear a potato sack and look way better than good in public.

There was something to be said for a luxury car. Actually, if

Teresa were honest with herself, there was something to be said for butlers, and cooks, and maids, and a plethora of other luxuries that came with the Baron lifestyle.

"You doing okay?" Cooper asked her for the umpteenth time since they'd left the ranch.

"Just enjoying the drive." Turning her head, she smiled at him. The last thing she wanted him to know was every time he got too close to the car in front of them, her whole body tensed. Probably survival instincts after having been smashed into by a red light runner. Time, she hoped, would wipe away the jitters. "I don't know if every twenty-four hours I'm going to feel way better than the day before, or if just getting out of that hospital where they wake you up every five minutes to ask if you're sleeping was all I needed to feel better."

"You do look better rested." He returned his attention to the road. "I asked Eve where she thought was the best place to get what you need and she suggested the Woodlands mall. It's huge and has a little of everything."

Familiar with the mall, she had to agree with Eve for selection, but the huge part was a little disconcerting. Even though she felt more rested today than yesterday, and had dropped the dosage on her pain meds since the surgery almost a week ago, walking all over the mall held as much appeal as eating chocolate covered ants.

"She also suggested we borrow a wheelchair. Otherwise your doctor will have a lot to say to me for pushing you too hard."

"I do not need a wheelchair."

Slowing for a red light, he turned to face her and didn't look away.

"Okay. Maybe I shouldn't walk too much, but I don't need a wheelchair."

The man did not say a word. He just continued to look at her, one eyebrow just a smidge higher than the other.

Apparently in all these years, some things didn't change. His gaze spoke volumes, and even in high school, that look was all he needed to win an argument. Of course, the way the butterflies in her stomach took to swooshing about might have helped his winning odds. "What if I walk till I'm tired and then if we haven't found enough, I get a wheelchair?"

The light turned green and he stepped on the gas. "Were you always this stubborn in high school?"

Her cheeks pulled hard on her lips. "I learned from the best."

"I beg your pardon." He shot her a brief sideways glance, but she could see the humor in his eyes.

"If the shoe fits…"

A deep laugh rumbled through the car. "Touché. More than one person may have mentioned the stubborn streak in Baron genetics."

Relaxing against the headrest, she had to smile. There was much to be said for Baron genetics. Considering she knew nothing about her own, there had to be some comfort in knowing where you came from. A comfort Emma probably wouldn't have.

"You're awfully quiet."

"Just resting before the big expedition."

A low chuckle sounded. "Hate to ask what you'd call climbing up Mt. Everest."

"Insanity."

Again, he burst out laughing. "I sure have missed you."

Her eyes popped open wide and her head snapped to face him. It certainly looked like he was sincere and not simply being polite. She would have sworn that after he graduated, he never gave her another thought. Oh, how she'd missed having him around those not so hallowed halls. It was sort of taken for granted around school that he was like her big brother. If anyone messed with her, they'd have to deal with the Barons. By the time she graduated three years later, most folks didn't remember she'd been chummy with a Baron until he'd heard she wasn't planning on attending her prom and offered to escort her. Dancing with him had probably been the most fun she'd ever had in her life. But it wasn't just his kind heart and the sense of security she'd missed, it was that twinkle in his eye and easy laugh that always made her want to laugh too. And there wasn't much in her life in those days that made her want to laugh. "Ditto."

"Here we are." Pulling into the mall, he frowned at the spaces and then sighed. "I'm going to drop you off at the door. No point in losing precious energy crossing the parking lot."

"Agreed. I'll find a bench and wait for you inside."

Considering he found at her at the bench mere moments after she'd sat down, she didn't know if that meant she was moving that slowly, or if he'd parachuted in from the parking lot.

"Shall we?" He extended his elbow to her.

Knee-jerk reaction had been to grumble she didn't need help, but that familiar winsome smile had her accepting the gesture and within minutes, darn grateful. Strolling the mall on his arm was not only more fun, it was easier than walking on her own steam. The first stop was a discount store with lots of casual clothes in the window. In less than two minutes and a few steps, she was able to survey the store from where she stood and shook her head.

"You don't want to look around?"

She sighed. "Nope."

With a shrug, he led her out the door and strolling down a few more stores, pointed to one with a few dresses in the window.

Again she shook her head. "Those are linen. Great for work if you have stock in a dry-cleaning company."

"You don't think there's some other dresses inside?"

"Doubtful." Under normal circumstances she'd have gone in just in case, but knowing her ability to walk on her own steam was going to be limited, she passed.

Another few stores and she stopped in her tracks.

"What?"

"In here." Granted the Hawaiian-themed shirts hanging in the storefront weren't exactly what she'd been looking for, but she couldn't resist. "Everyone needs a little sunshine in their lives."

"Sunshine?" Rolling his eyes, he followed her in. The expression on his face teetering between horrified and confused made her want to laugh.

"Isn't this cute?" She held up a button-down shirt that was more suitable for a stroll on a Caribbean beach than a day on a ranch.

"That's a man's shirt."

She had to bite down on her lower lip to control her smile. "I know."

"You won't wear a man's t-shirt, but you want to wear a man's Hawaiian shirt?"

Shaking her head, she let the smile bloom.

"Oh, no." His eyes widened, his head shifted left to right and his hands shot up, palms out. "Absolutely not."

"But it would bring out the green in your eyes." She did her best to keep a straight face.

His eyes narrowed, and the horror was replaced with determination.

Uh-oh. She recognized that look. It was the same look he'd had after a school car wash fundraiser and she'd accidentally sprayed him with the hose. That original transgression quickly forgiven, but when she did it again just to get a rise out of him, that same look in his eyes had appeared and the two of them wound up doused with water more than any of the cars. They'd also laughed till their sides hurt. She wasn't so sure about right now.

Turning his back on her, he pushed a few items around on a nearby rack and spun about, grinning like the village fool. "Perfect."

The sight of the olive-green palm leaves plastered all over the cotton dress with bold red strokes of what might have been bird feathers left her stunned. Or perhaps—if he was serious—panicked.

"We'll match." He looked down at the lime-green shirt in her hand and over to his colorful choice for her and added, "Almost."

The next words out of their mouths came in choreographed unison. "Dare you."

Instantly they both broke out laughing, only she had to drop the shirt and use both arms to wrap around her middle. "Ouch," she winced, struggling to contain her mirth.

"You're not supposed to make me laugh."

If the dress he'd held had been on fire, he couldn't have dropped it any faster. "Oh, Lord, I'm sorry. Are you okay?"

Nodding, she sucked in a deep breath, then bit back another smile. "Maybe I was a little hasty." She grabbed the nearest floral shirt. "How do you feel about blue?"

CHAPTER ELEVEN

Cooper couldn't remember the last time he'd enjoyed shopping as much as he had with Tess several days ago. At one point, he was afraid to even look at her for fear they'd both burst into laughter and send her doubled over in pain again. In the end, they did indeed buy matching Hawaiian outfits, but nothing as bold as the first outrageous ones they'd pulled out.

By the time Tess was running out of steam, they'd managed to purchase several comfy dresses. Apparently, cotton comfort was in fashion this season. She bought a few short sleeve dresses, a few sleeveless, and all of them looked fabulous on her. Though she'd only tried on a couple. It hadn't occurred to either of them that getting in and out of clothes would be exhausting for her, and a bit uncomfortable. He knew she was trying her best to hide the discomfort, but he could read it in her eyes as easily as he could have read her name on a driver's license.

"It's time to see Mama." He unsnapped the straps on the car seat.

Grinning up at him, Emma kicked her feet and contentedly squealed, "Mama!"

He knew exactly how the kid felt. Ever since leaving the house with Emma, as he'd done every day this week, all he could think about was coming back to the ranch and seeing Tess again. Lifting Emma out of the seat, he kissed her temple and when her arms flew around his neck and squeezed tightly, he couldn't help but squeeze her back. The routine had become so natural, he couldn't remember a time when things were any different. First he'd rise and get dressed before seeing to Emma. Then they would join her mother for breakfast.

At first they would meet in the dining room so that Emma wouldn't see Tess struggling with going down the stairs. With each day, Tess's mobility improved and the last couple of days, she'd meet them by the changing table and help get Emma ready for her day. After breakfast he would take Emma to daycare so that Tess wouldn't have to strain herself. Not that his grandparents and the staff would allow her to, but still, as long as Emma was happy at daycare, it made the most sense.

Trotting up the front steps, with Emma still holding on to his neck, he didn't have to bother with the front door, Jeeves had it open and waiting for him.

"Miss Teresa is in the parlor waiting." Jeeves leaned into him slightly and lowered his voice. "She's been working all afternoon, sir, and talking with Miss Katrina."

Stubborn was the first word that came to mind. "Thank you for letting me know."

Since Tess had come home, she'd insisted she was at least capable of doing some work from the recliner on a laptop. He'd thought he'd won the battle of she should fully recover, but apparently, he'd underestimated her determination. He really should have known better.

To his surprise, rather than find Tess on the recliner waiting for her little girl, she was approaching the entry to the family's gathering room. "Hello, baby!"

Emma perked up, her grin wide as the Rio Grande and smart little girl that she was, she opened her arms to hug her mama but didn't pull away for Tess to hold her. Every single day this child's intuitive understanding amazed him.

"You're looking good." He heard his own words and panic struck. "I mean, not that you don't always look good... I mean, it's just... you look stronger, like you're feeling better."

Not bothering to hide her mirth at his stumbling over his own words, Tess chuckled softly. "I feel a lot better. I think sitting around waiting wasn't doing me any favors. I got with Katrina today and she sent me some preliminary docs to review and help me get a feel for what's going on."

"And?"

"To be determined. There's a lot to take in, but I already have a few ideas spinning around in my head to streamline a few procedures. I noticed a crossover of replication in processes, but I need to stew on it a bit. See how things can better fit in the time-box."

"Just don't push too hard."

"I won't. But I was thinking. Since I'm walking and feeling better, I thought Emma might enjoy a visit to the stables."

"You think you're really up to it?" *Go ahead, pea brain, doubt the smartest woman you ever met.* "Never mind. I think it's a great idea. I bet there's even a foal or calf in the barn. This time of year there usually is."

Her hand touched his arm and he could have sworn the heat seared his skin. "It's okay. I really am feeling much better. And you don't have to worry about every word you say. I knew what you meant."

At least someone knew what he meant, because right about now, he was pretty confused about what he was thinking and feeling. Hefting Emma tightly in one arm, he waved toward the back door with the other.

"Up me down." Emma wiggled in his grip. Tess was right, it was going to be a sorry day when she stopped saying that.

Letting her down, he assumed she was going to want her mother to pick her up, but still holding on to his hand, she scrambled close to her mother and snatched hold of her hand too. The good thing was that Emma's toddler pace was in line with Tess' recovering pace. The downside was that as much as he loved—to his surprise truly loved—holding little Emma's hand and spending time with her, right now, he really wished it was Tess's hand he got to hold. Maybe what he needed to do was find a time, sooner than later, when he could do just that.

★

Was it silly of Teresa to wish that she could walk holding Cooper's hand? Heaven knew all through their high school friendship, she'd longed for a chance to walk holding hands, but those were teenage daydreams laced with a vivid imagination, well grounded in the impossible fairy tale and the elusive happily ever after. From the time she was a young child, for as long as she could remember, she longed for a real family of her own. One that sat down to dinner every night at an actual table and who helped with homework and took summer vacations and visited grandma and grandpa for Christmas. At some point those daydreams of wishful thinking shifted focus on one man. Eventually, she grew up and learned to focus her efforts on the real world.

When Mr. Right failed to make an appearance, she went ahead with her life's dream of having her own family. Even before she got pregnant with Emma, Teresa had planned her little family's future. Emma would never want for her mother's love or time.

"You look awfully serious." Cooper slid the barn door open.

"Horsey!" Emma squealed with glee, her little arm pointing at a horse hanging his head over the stall door.

"Yes." Teresa squeezed her daughter's hand. "A real horsey." Looking up, she smiled at Cooper.

Cooper returned the smile. "Looks like you were right."

Emma tugged hard until their hold on her hands broke free as she darted toward the horse.

"Whoa, little one." Cooper reached her daughter in two long strides and scooping her up, slid her onto his shoulders. "We don't run up to horses. We have to approach slowly. Not fast. We don't want to scare the horse, right?"

She frowned a minute and then sighed as though she'd considered his words and relented, having decided that she did not want to scare the horse more than she wanted to run to the massive animal. Which, Teresa did not understand why the inbred instinct for self-preservation hadn't kicked in and kept Emma cautiously at her mother's side.

Pausing by the tack room door, Cooper reached into a

small bucket and dropped some treats into his pockets, holding one in his hand. "Do you want to feed the horsey?"

Two little feet kicked into his shoulders as she bounced in place. "Horsey."

Cooper chuckled and looked to Teresa. "One track mind. She most definitely inherited your focused determination."

Chuckling, Teresa shook her head. "I wouldn't mind if she did indeed inherit a determined gene, but I suspect this is nothing more than two-year-old jubilance at something new."

Opening his hand, palm open and flat with a treat in place, Cooper fed the horse and Emma giggled. He did it one more time before asking Emma if she wanted to feed the animal.

"Yes." Her little head bobbed and golden locks bounced at the nape of her neck. An ache pricked at Teresa over how fast her little one was growing.

When he placed a treat into Emma's hand, even though Teresa knew the horses weren't dangerous, she also knew they had big teeth, Emma had little hands, and two-year-olds weren't always very good at following rules. "Uh. Are you sure this is a good idea?"

His smile seared her like a surgical laser. "It will be fine."

"I don't know, she's awfully young."

"Horsey. Feed horsey."

Teresa sighed and leveled her gaze with Cooper's. "Are you sure, you're sure?"

His head bobbed and she returned the nod, and like she'd done every day since Emma was born, prayed for God to watch over her.

To Teresa's relief, Cooper set the treat in her daughter's hand. Then, holding her hand in his, he eased her hand in front of the horse and held it steady.

The horse seemed to sniff at the air before ever so gently nipping the treat out of the little cherub's hand. It was no surprise to Teresa when the horse's lips tickled Emma's palm, making her laugh.

Fingertips pursed together, Emma tapped the tips together and called out, "More."

Cooper gave her another treat for the horse and again guided her through feeding the animal.

To Teresa, the scene was perfect. Her daughter was thrilled, she was regaining her strength, and Cooper was every bit the perfect father figure she'd always thought he would become. How could anyone come from such a loving and caring family and not be good parenting material? After all, he'd had excellent examples from his parents to his grandparents. Of course, no matter what her drug-induced dreams might have been or what Emma's birth certificate said, this loving family scenario would be over soon. Too soon.

Lifting Emma off of his shoulder and setting her down on the ground, Cooper took her daughter's hand and with Emma at his left, he leaned right, closer to Teresa. "Are you feeling okay? Should we go back?"

Obviously, he'd confused her thoughtful expression for one of discomfort. Though the whole situation was indeed a bit uncomfortable, it had nothing to do with her physical recovery. "Sorry. Lost in thought."

"You've been doing that a lot lately."

Emma tugged at his hand and urged him to move forward to another stall. Cooper led her all the way down to a birthing stall where a calf was curled up in a corner while its mother munched on a snack. While he squatted down beside his charge and the calf, Emma gently pet the baby cow, Cooper looked up at Tess. "Still have that sweet tooth?"

"Is the pope Catholic," she deadpanned, a sly smile immediately blooming on her face.

"So, what you're saying is once we put Emma down for the night, it wouldn't take much to talk you into going with me to Alamode for an ice cream?"

"You mean the mom and pop joint we always went to for a little peace and quiet while studying and the best homemade ice cream this side of the Mississippi is still in business?"

"Even the pandemic couldn't kill people's love of good ice cream."

There was no way on earth she was skipping out on going anywhere with Cooper. Trying not to grin like a teenager invited to prom by the captain of the football team, she took in a deep breath and nodded. "You're on."

CHAPTER TWELVE

The last thing Cooper had expected to do this evening was to find himself on the road to Alamode with Tess. Not till he'd heard the words come out of his mouth did he know what he'd been thinking.

"I wonder if they still serve butter pecan." Her head tilted back against the headrest and her eyes closed, a slight smile rested on Tess's lips.

"I bet they do. It's as much a staple in the ice cream world as vanilla and chocolate."

"Do you remember the first time you brought me there?"

He remembered a lot of things about Tess. More than she probably knew. "I'd gotten an A-minus on my physics test. We went to celebrate. After that it became a regular study hang out."

"I still have the extra poundage on my hips to prove it," she chuckled, then sighed. "I was so surprised by that first invitation, but I was even more surprised by the little ice cream parlor. I guess I expected people as rich as the Barons to only eat at fancy places."

"Ah." He bobbed his head. "The born with a silver spoon in the mouth thing."

"Well," her hands twisted in her lap, "Y'all do have silver all over that dining room."

All right. He couldn't argue with her there. The family really did eat with sterling silver flatware. And a few other sterling service pieces. All he could do was shrug. "I honestly hadn't thought that Mr. Wingate was going to pass me even if I got 100% on every test, but I knew if I could keep up those grades for the rest of the tests, I stood a really good chance."

"You sang."

"I what?" The memory of it was coming back. He'd started out tapping his high school ring on the steering wheel, and by the time they'd parked their car at the mom-and-pop ice cream parlor on an old Texas Farm Road, he'd exited the car singing Frank Sinatra's popular tune "I Get a Kick out of You." He'd been so darn thankful for her patience with him. She'd proven to be so much more than just a freshman who was good at math and physics. She was understanding, patient, and when she allowed herself to speak her mind, had a cutting sense of humor. She didn't let him get away with anything and he very much appreciated that. Other than coming up with the nickname Princess Tess to offset her dismal sense of self-worth from having grown up without parents, he never did tell her just how much he thought of her back then. Though, right about now, if he sang the song to her, it would be for totally different reasons than gratitude. Wincing, he shook his head ever so slightly. If he were honest with himself, even back then it was most likely about more than gratitude. "I probably sang it flat and off-key."

"You sounded lovely. I thought it was wonderful and quite sweet."

"Sweet, huh?" Just what every man wants to hear.

She shrugged. "Honestly, up until that day, I was a little intimidated by the whole Baron legacy."

"Really?" His heart dived. Had he been the reason she initially had been so shy and soft-spoken, almost beaten down?

She nodded. "Aside from the overall intimidating factor of the Baron name in general, aside from the fact that we had the best public high school in the state thanks to all the years of Baron subsidies and donations, you were a high-and-mighty senior and I was a very lowly freshman."

His mind scrambled to remember if he'd ever said or done anything rude or off-putting, but he was drawing a blank. "Did I make you feel that way?"

The chuckle that accompanied the soft scoff wasn't helping his concerns. "Never. From the minute you sat down at the table in front of me and declared you sucked at physics, I knew you were not the arrogant image I'd created in my mind. You were nothing but polite and considerate, which was a total surprise since most of the seniors teased the freshman in some way or other and a few were down right bullies."

"But before knowing me, were you afraid of me?" That whole concept really bothered him. He didn't like the idea of anyone being afraid of him, especially not Tess, and not for even a second.

"Afraid is a little strong. You were handsome, friendly, popular, and rich. You ran with the in crowd, not the smart geeks. Anyone with those credentials would have been intimidating, but from that first telling declaration, I knew you were actually a nice guy, and once you ordered the dreamsicle flavored ice cream and dug into it like a little kid, all the trappings fell away and I realized, your last name didn't make a—no pun intended—lick of difference. And then, once I met your family, I realized the acorn didn't fall far from the tree. Everyone was always warm and welcoming and caring and never judgmental. I always felt safe with your family."

Safe. Oh, how he hated the idea that she'd ever not felt safe anywhere else. If something as simple as eating ice cream had …"Wait, you remembered the flavor I picked?"

Eyes widening for just a moment, she blew out a sigh and shrugged. "It seemed like something a little kid would ask for, and you really did eat it with a lot of gusto."

"I'm not fond of melting ice cream dripping everywhere."

"Maybe," she hefted that one shoulder again, "but to me it looked like you were thoroughly enjoying your dessert."

Now he hefted a shoulder. Dreamsicle anything was his weakness. He'd loved the flavor even as a young boy and had never outgrown it. Pulling into the small parking lot in front of the old clapboard framed house, he scurried around to open her door.

Standing by the car, Tess tipped her head back just a bit and her gaze surveyed the old white building in front of her. "It's amazing how so much in the world is changing at the speed of light, and yet, some things stay exactly the same as we remember them."

"Nice, isn't it?" He extended his elbow to her, delighted when she slowly slipped her hand into the curve of his arm.

"Why, if it isn't Cooper Baron as I live and breathe." Gertie Madison had to be as old as his grandmother on a good day, and like Grams, as sharp as a tack and fit as a fiddle, with a memory that didn't quit.

"In the flesh. How ya doing, Gertie?"

Waving an ice cream scoop in the air, Gertie smiled. "If I can't complain, then it's a good day." Gertie's gaze settled on Tess and her eyes narrowed, then her brows shot up and a smile took over her face. "Teresa. Well, isn't this a nice surprise. Good to see both of you. One dreamsicle and one butter pecan?"

This lady had a memory like a steel trap. Not a lick of rust anywhere. He turned to Tess and caught her nodding at Gertie.

"Sounds good," Cooper concurred, handing the lady a few bills. "Two double scoop cones, please."

Her back to them, Gertie bent over and started scooping the creamy confection. "I would have expected to see you here with children in tow by now."

Tess beamed. "Emma's asleep, but now that I know you're still here I'll have to bring her. She's not quite two but already loves ice cream."

Scooper in hand, Gertie spun about and grinned. "I'm glad to see you two finally figured it out."

Figured it out? The old woman's words bounced around in Teresa's mind.

"I always thought you two were so cute together. And so well balanced. Y'all complemented each other beautifully. I bet you've made beautiful babies."

There was little doubt in Teresa's mind from the heat creeping up inside her that her cheeks were now bright pink. "Oh, no."

"What?" Gertie handed Teresa her cone. "Your baby isn't beautiful?"

"No, I mean, yes, Emma is very beautiful. And sweet too."

"Thought so." Gertie turned back around and reached into a different tub.

Closing his eyes, Cooper barely shook his head before opening them again. Leaning into her, he softly whispered, "Confusing me for Emma's father seems to be a theme."

"I'm sorry," she whispered back, returning her attention to Gertie. "Emma is my little girl. Not Cooper's."

The woman handed him his ice cream. "That's okay. Sometimes it takes a few mistakes to recognize what you had all along. Now, enjoy your ice cream."

All set to explain that she and Cooper weren't a couple, then or now, Teresa stared at Gertie's back disappearing through a door by the counter. Now what?

"Your ice cream is melting."

Snapping her jaw shut, her gaze dropped to the cone in her hand that was indeed melting, then darted up to Cooper. The man was licking his ice cream. What she didn't know or understand was why was he smiling.

Leaning forward, he stuck out his tongue and licked a drop dripping down the side of her cone. "Delicious." He straightened. "You'd better start eating."

Not sure she could handle watching Cooper lick at her ice cream cone again, she quickly licked at each drop of ice cream making its way down the side of the cone and then glanced up at him. "How can you be smiling? Gertie thinks you're Emma's father."

"I've had people think worse things about me."

She could feel her eyes bugging out of their sockets.

"Relax. I'm getting used to people assuming she's mine. Gertie is harmless. It's not like she works for a national news network."

He probably had a point, but that still didn't explain why the whole jumping to conclusion thing didn't phase him.

His hand at the small of her back, Cooper urged her across the small shop toward a small iron table and chairs. "Is this okay?"

"Perfect."

The man actually pulled her chair out. In an ice cream parlor. Always the gentleman. Her mind flew back to the school study rooms for tutors. She was pretty sure there wasn't a single session where he didn't pull her chair out for her. It was kind of nice knowing that it was a habit he hadn't broken or outgrown.

"I truly believe this is still the best butter pecan ice cream on the planet."

"You're not going to get an argument from me. Though I am going to make it a point to come by more often. I suspect when my grandfather reminds me that life is short, enjoy the small gifts life brings us, I do believe he's talking about Gertie's ice cream."

"Brings back so many memories of when life was just simpler."

"I don't remember you having a simple life."

She shrugged. "Others had it worse. Especially once your family got involved. I can't imagine how hard it would have been to get through college on my own."

"You were brilliant, it wouldn't be hard."

"I didn't mean academically. At eighteen we're booted out of where we live and our foster families take in someone new to replace us." She wasn't going to say to replace their income loss. "So many kids literally are on the street with a sack of clothes and nowhere to go and a grim future. It could have easily been me."

"I'm glad it wasn't." He stopped licking his cone and stared into her eyes. "If my family had anything to do with making your life in college easier, I'm very glad."

She actually rolled her eyes at him. "The scholarship the Baron family established for foster kids made everything possible for me, and for so many smart foster kids after me."

His head bobbed, and he swallowed a lick of his ice cream. "What happened?"

Tilting her head slightly, she studied him.

"I remember you sharing your dreams of a big happy family. Something about a good man, a good job, and comfortable shoes." He bit back a smile. "Why did you decide to have a baby on your own?"

"Around my twenty-eighth birthday, a coworker went on maternity leave. When the baby was about a month old, Carol brought her daughter in to meet everyone."

"Let me guess, the whole office stopped and everyone came around to coo and tickle the bundle of joy."

"Pretty much, but for me, it reminded me that while I was making a good career for myself, and had plenty of comfortable shoes, that good man was still quite elusive. My whole life I'd dreamed of a family of my own, and if I didn't stop and spend some of the time I spent on my career on finding that man, I'd miss out completely."

Cooper nodded and took a last lick of his ice cream before munching on the cone and chucking his napkins into a nearby trash bin.

"By the time my thirtieth birthday rolled around, I realized I was running out of time to have a family of my own. I looked into artificial insemination and decided, if other women could be single moms, so could I."

"Now, you're a family of two."

"I don't want her to be an only child. I don't want her alone when I'm gone. I don't want the burden of my old age landing solely on her shoulders. I hope to have more."

"If they're as sweet and perfect as Emma, you should have a dozen."

Her cheeks tugged at the corners of her mouth. "Funny, that's what I was thinking."

CHAPTER THIRTEEN

One thing in Cooper's life was guaranteed, his grandmother was never to be underestimated. Expecting Margaret to bring him his coffee before Emma awoke, as the maid had done for weeks, this morning, after a rap on his door, Margaret informed him that his grandmother had gotten Emma up and was already downstairs enjoying breakfast with the child.

"A travesty." The Governor held a folded newspaper in his hand and was tapping at it with one finger. "It's a miracle no one was hurt."

Standing at the buffet pouring a cup of coffee, Devlin shook his head. "I barely got any sleep following the breaking newscasts."

Without his coffee, Cooper was finding it hard to follow the conversation. Pouring his own cup, it dawned on him that his brother had not been there last night when they'd all gone to bed. "What time did you get here?"

"Little after seven."

"Last night?" That made no sense.

"This morning." Setting down the slice of toast he'd just slathered with an inch of marmalade, Devlin stopped and waved a couple of fingers at Emma seated between him and their grandmother. "I thought it was time to visit with my niece again."

"She's not your niece." Though, ever since ice cream the other night, he'd found himself more than once distracted by thoughts of Tess and wishing he'd paid more attention to the passing of time and looked her up before their pinky swear deadline had come and gone.

"Could have fooled me," Devlin continued to entertain

Emma, "she has your eyes."

"Lots of people have green eyes. As a matter of fact, so do you." That got his brother straightening in his seat.

"Don't look at me. I haven't seen Teresa since you were in high school."

"Ditto." He forced a toothy smile at his brother.

"A simple DNA test would solve this argument." Their grandmother flashed a sweet smile that completely contradicted the depth of her statement.

"Grams," he and Devlin echoed simultaneously.

Cooper shot his brother a look and turned his attention back to his grandmother. "Grams, I explained to you. I haven't seen Tess since her high school graduation." His grandmother should know, she'd insisted most of the Baron clan attend to cheer the first recipient of the Baron Foster System Collegiate Scholarship.

"Yes, dear." The sweet smile remained intact and he was pretty sure the woman's mind remained unconvinced that he couldn't possibly be Emma's father.

"Family is more than blood," the Governor muttered, shaking his head at the newspaper that occupied his thoughts. "Contractors who cut corners to save a buck should all be flogged, then tarred and feathered."

"We ran into something similar with that mall project in East Texas about five years ago. One of the construction workers anonymously reported the concrete contractor for using recycled concrete. Had he gotten away with it we could have had a complete collapse of that underground garage. What a nightmare that would have been."

Meanwhile, Cooper still wasn't sure exactly what they were talking about. "Now that I've had a few sips of my morning caffeine jolt, anyone care to update me on exactly what has everyone all riled up?"

Devlin sighed, and if Cooper wasn't mistaken, growled under his breath before speaking. "The central tower on that new multi-use project south of downtown collapsed. The first tenants were set to move in tomorrow. Had the dang thing taken two more days to implode, who knows how many people would have been injured or killed."

"With all the permits and inspections and hoops we have to go through, how the hell does something like this still happen?" Now Cooper was all riled up and suddenly realized, little Emma was following the conversation like a spectator at a tennis match, and taking in every word. He was going to have to watch his language no matter how irritated he was over the situation.

"Perhaps we're jumping to conclusions?" Grams suggested sweetly.

The Governor shook his head. "Not possible. Buildings properly constructed with approved product do not suddenly fall down."

"That's what I'm afraid of." Cooper hated stories like this. "That some engineer, contractor, or project manager put profit above human lives is enough to make my skin crawl."

"Agreed." The Governor reached over to pet one of the dogs. Pausing to form his words. "It has to be either gleaning the budget using underrated product, or human-cut corners on the process to save a dime or two, or outright using inferior product."

"Thank heaven we don't have to worry about any of our contractors." That much Cooper was sure of. He hoped.

Dressed in an eye-catching light blue top and cropped tan pants, Tess entered the dining room, stepped aside to give her daughter a quick morning kiss between Emma's bites of bacon and scrambled eggs, then straightened and looking Cooper in the eye, sighed. "I wouldn't hold my breath on that one."

Teresa was all for saving money through efficiency and use of innovative superior products that cut down on potential maintenance, but two things rubbed her the wrong way: replacing the human touch with technology, and skimping to save a dime. She hadn't said anything to Cooper yet, not till she could be more certain. Yesterday her doctor had cleared her to drive and today she had every intention of checking things out in person.

"What do you mean?" His gaze narrowed, Cooper looked up at her from his seat at the table.

"I heard about the accident. Started digging around a bit online. There's still limited info, but I called a former coworker this morning to find out what the inside word is and I got the name of the concrete contractor. Manning Brothers seems to be leaving a trail of construction accidents in their wake."

His fork midair, Devlin set it back down. "They're on the short list for a new development I'm working on."

His lips tightened into a thin line, Cooper sucked in a deep breath. "Is this rumor or do we have proof?"

"They hide their tracks well." Teresa sighed. "A few projects ago, I got some anonymous tips that there were short cuts being taken. There was a bonus involved for every day the project completed ahead of schedule."

Both Cooper and Devlin nodded.

"We give similar incentives from time to time." Cooper turned to his brother, who was still bobbing his head. "I don't think we ever considered it could also be an incentive to cut corners."

Teresa nodded. "Which is why no one at my former company blinked an eye when the contractor ran day-and-night crews to save time."

Now Cooper shook his head. "I don't think I'm going to like where this is going."

"Exactly." She sat down with her coffee and an English muffin. "The materials used during the day fully met the safety specs set out by the engineers. The night crew was a different story. My coworker and I headed out one night just for a spot inspection. There was scrambling and excuses, and delays and we knew something wasn't right. Next time we went a tad more stealthily. Parked down the road." She paused and smiled. "Hate to admit it, but we wore black clothes and snuck around like a couple of thieves."

"And?"

"We found the recycled concrete they were using. I

took videos, photos, ordered construction halted, and after the firestorm was over, we had a new concrete contractor involved and took a financial hit removing and redoing the foundation work Manning had already done. Thankfully, they hadn't gotten further, but, of course, part of the settling included a gag order."

"Which you're not keeping." Devlin smiled up at her.

She shrugged. "I didn't sign anything, and I don't work for the company anymore, and more importantly, guess who has the concrete contract for the new project I'm overseeing."

Cooper closed his eyes for a second and blew out a deep sigh. "Manning Brothers."

Putting her finger on the tip of her nose, she nodded. "Ding ding ding. Give the man a prize."

"I'll talk to legal. See what we can do." Cooper shook his head and sighed.

Her heart swelled that Cooper was willing to take action on her word and her word alone.

"You're going to need more proof." The Governor turned to Teresa. "Not that we don't believe you, we do, but if this character wants to get ugly, we're going to need a paper trail."

"I know. I've already started putting one together. And thank you for your confidence. When I'd approached my former boss, he practically ignored me. Finally relenting if I got one of the male project managers involved."

"Construction is still considered a man's world in many ways." Cooper shook his head. "I'm sorry that happened."

"It happens a lot." Devlin added. "I've fired more than one really good crew member for how they treated the women on the site. We don't have a lot of female construction workers, but when they put on a hard hat and swing a hammer, they become one of the team and deserve the same respect the men get."

"Good for you." A smile took over Mrs. Baron's face.

In her youth, Tess hadn't met a Baron she didn't like, and from what she'd seen since her accident, not a single one seems to have grown into an idiot. She admired every one, especially Cooper. Where he was involved, that hint of a schoolgirl crush she shared with half the female students was quickly blooming into something much more complex. At least for her.

"What happens now?" the Governor asked.

All heads turned in his direction. After a long moment of silence, and his gaze clearly settling on Teresa, she hefted one shoulder and stood for more coffee. "Basic recognizance today. I need to see where things are at in person, not just on paper, and I need to dig around and see what else is happening in the rumor mills. I suspect strongly there will be a lot of noise after yesterday's collapse."

"Get the phone number for Carter Gibbs from Katrina. He's been grumbling about Manning in Dallas. He might have some key insights for you. Honestly, I didn't pay enough attention to him because of Manning's good reputation, but now I'm wishing I had. Promise me one thing, whatever you do," Cooper's expression turned serious, "do not take any action until we've had a chance to sit down and hash out our options. I've learned from experience that men cornered like trapped rats can be unpredictable and much more dangerous. I do not, under any circumstances, want you caught in the crossfire."

"I can—"

He held up his hand, cutting her off. "That wasn't a suggestion. I know you are very competent, it's why we hired you, but some risks aren't worth taking. Am I clear?"

As much as she hated being treated like a girl, she knew deep down that Cooper would take that same concerned tone with a man, and nodded her head. And maybe, just maybe, she'd allow herself the illusion that his concern for her was more than employer to employee. Wouldn't that be something?

CHAPTER FOURTEEN

Every minute of the day, Cooper resisted the urge to call Tess and check up on her. He could not remember a time in his life when he was so worried about someone. A feeling deep in his gut told him that this whole concrete contractor thing was not going to be simple or easy. He'd checked with his lawyers and they were now reviewing the contracts that Cooper signed for an escape clause, but his new project manager's views were not due cause. If that wasn't enough, he was concerned that she'd overdo her first day back on the job.

As it is, he and his grandparents had to argue for her to remain at the house until her doctor gave her the all clear to lift Emma. Tess had argued she could figure something out and the family had rebutted that it wasn't necessary to risk her health. If there was anything he'd figured out about Tess, it was that she had a determination that teetered on hardheaded stubbornness.

Now his gut was twisting and he didn't like it one bit. Pushing the phone toggle on his steering wheel, he called Katrina's direct line. "Hey."

"I was wondering when you were going to check in." He could hear Katrina typing as she spoke to him. "Our phone has been ringing off the wall. Anyone would think that collapse last night was one of our properties."

"Learn anything other than what's being reported on the news?"

"Yeah. Half the city inspectors and engineers are wanting outside collaboration."

"Collaboration?"

Katrina sighed. "That's the modern vernacular for they

want to cover their asses and get nongovernment engineers to help with the investigation."

That shouldn't have surprised him, but it did. "Anything more?"

"Yes. You're at the top of their short list. I've let everyone know I would have you get back to them if you can clear your schedule."

If he got involved, that would certainly provide him the ammunition he needed for just cause to terminate the contract with Manning Brothers. "I'll make some phone calls. In the meantime, any news from the newbie?" He hoped that came out as casual as he'd tried to make it sound.

"You mean Teresa?"

"How many other newbies do we have?" For years, he'd called every other recent hire *newbie*, but from the sound of Katrina's voice, maybe his effort to pretend Tess was just another new hire whose kid he happened to be helping care for was pushing his luck.

"Just asking." Was that a smile he heard in her voice now, or was he being paranoid that everyone around him knew how he felt about Tess. And how did he feel? Would he be this worried if Gibbs were on a hunt for incriminating evidence? What about his other employees with medical restrictions? Shaking his head, he did his best to wrap his mind around all the feelings churning inside him. Sugarcoat it any way he wanted, the bottom line was that he was most definitely falling hard for his Princess Tess.

"Earth to Cooper," Katrina practically shouted.

"What?" Lord, kicking around his thoughts of Tess, he hadn't heard a word Katrina had said.

"I said that she called earlier asking for Gibbs's contact info but I informed her that he had to take a few days off for his grandmother's funeral."

Blast. Firstly, how did he not know the man had lost a family member? Cooper would be a basket case when his grandmother's time came; but secondly, he did not want Tess facing down Manning on her own.

"You still with me?"

"Yes. Thinking about the concrete contracts for the new hospital project."

"That's what Teresa said. She seemed less than pleased when I told her that the project is ahead of schedule."

"Wait, how did I not hear about this?"

He could almost hear Katrina rolling her eyes on the other end of the line. "Probably because you've been more preoccupied with the daughter that isn't your daughter than with reading my memos. They're getting ready to start pouring today."

"Does Tess know?"

"You mean Teresa? Yes. I told her when she called."

Dang it. "Okay, thanks. I'll check in with her."

"You do that." Katrina muttered something else before disconnecting the call.

Glancing at the clock, he really hoped that Tess was heading back to the office and not the construction site, but somehow he doubted that. Hitting the phone button again, he pulled into a nearby parking lot and called her. The phone rang once and then went to voice mail. Not what he wanted. Dialing again, he listened to her voice message and blew out a sigh. Throwing his work truck in gear, he pulled out of the parking lot, his tires screeching behind him.

Even though he had no idea if Tess was confronting Manning or on her way to the office or going back to the ranch, he was heading to the construction site. The knots that had been twisting in his gut were now tightening like wet rope and his blood pressure was definitely climbing. He had to get to Tess sooner than later.

Turning onto the freeway and heading south, he tried dialing one more time. Same as the time before, the phone went straight to voicemail. "Come on, Tess. Why aren't you answering?"

From the minute Katrina informed Teresa that the hospital project was ahead of schedule, Teresa knew this was only the beginning of Manning's shenanigans. The wooden frames for the concrete weren't going to be a problem. Those would get removed after the concrete was poured regardless; her concern was the actual concrete. Even though she suspected the product poured in the daytime would meet the specs, she needed to stop this. Not that she had a clue how to do it.

Every time she tried to dial Cooper, his phone went straight to voicemail. She had no intention of leaving a message, she'd have to fill him in later. Showing her ID to the guard at the gate of the fenced in construction site, she proceeded to drive ahead, following the rumble of construction vehicles. In the distance she spotted the dust kicked up by the wheels of the cement truck.

Her car parked, Teresa slid out of her car, grabbed a hard hat from the back seat and desperately wished that she had worn steel toed shoes more suitable to the uneven terrain of the clumped Texas clay and the dangers of the surrounding heavy machinery. Her heart hammered in her chest as she strode across the construction site. Intent on keeping her balance despite her casual footwear, she kicked up dust with each determined step. The familiar rumble of the concrete truck spinning flamed her sense of urgency. She had to stop this before it got started.

Spotting a huddle of men around the massive footprint of wood framing, she redirected toward the crew. As soon as she had a clear view of the foundation, she immediately spotted the first problem. She didn't need to be a structural engineer to know there wasn't anywhere near enough rebar to reinforce the concrete. Not only was the man probably planning to use inferior concrete, he was pocketing money by skimping on the steel rods necessary to stop the concrete from crumbling years down the road. Any homeowner who had watched their driveway crack and lift had learned the hard way that not enough, or no rebar at all, had been used for the original pour.

"Who's in charge here?" she called out as loudly as she could over the rumble of the cement trucks lined up behind the crew.

No surprise that in the huddle of men, some holding shovels, others moving about in an effort to look busy, not a single one reacted to her.

Once again she called out, this time in Spanish, "Quien es el jefe?"

Now multiple heads turned to stare at her. One worker finally pointed to a gentleman in khaki slacks, his shirt sleeves rolled up, and a clipboard in hand as he seemed to be yelling at a guy actually dressed for work. Whether any of them had any intention of doing anything but watching she didn't know.

The man in the dress shirt spotted her, ending his tirade and shouting at her, "Lady, this is private property. What the hell do you think you're doing here?"

"Looking for the person in charge of those cement trucks." Her arm stuck straight out, her finger pointed in the direction of the trucks. In her peripheral vision, she spotted a third truck driving in from the main street. Was this character planning on pouring the whole site in a day? Who was she kidding? If he wanted to hide his rebar cut backs, he'd have to move fast.

"I'm with Baron Enterprises."

"This is no place for you to be gallivanting. Go back to your office." Without waiting for a response, he turned back to the guy in the yellow reflective jacket and hard hat to match.

"I'm not going anywhere until you send those trucks back where they came from."

"What the hell are you talking about?"

"I'm talking about the state investigating the collapse of the Preston Towers."

The man's eyes narrowed and the muscles in his jaw began to twitch. "What does that have to do with you stomping about my construction site in inappropriate attire?"

"Not a lick of concrete is to be poured until that investigation is over and your company is cleared of responsibility." She had to say that even though she knew there wouldn't be a snowball's chance in hell of him being cleared.

"Lady. Go home." Turning his back on her, he waved the first truck forward and returned his attention to the construction worker, probably the foreman, in front of him.

"You're not listening to me. Baron Enterprises does not want a single drop of concrete poured."

"I don't care what you say. I have a signed contract and a job to do and you are beginning to annoy me."

Standing just outside of swinging distance, not that she planned on slugging the guy but she wouldn't put it past him to take a swing at her, she widened her stance for better balance and one hand on her hips, the other pointed at the truck rumbling forward. "I haven't begun to annoy you. Stop the concrete trucks."

Almost smirking the guy shook his head and glared at her. "And who's going to make me? You?"

Oh, how she wished Cooper had answered the stupid phone. "You pour one drop of cement and you're going to find yourself on the wrong side of a very nasty lawsuit. Trust me, you do not want to go against the Baron family."

He took a step forward and stared her down.

It took an extra minute to tamp down the urge to step back and away from the guy's towering six foot plus frame.

"We'll see who sues who. Either you leave this site now, or I will have security toss you out on that pretty little ass of yours."

She hadn't expected the guy to be all sweet and rosy at her request, but she got the feeling that not only would he toss her out on her rear, he'd enjoy every minute of it. Screwing up her courage, she took a step forward. "Go ahead and try."

Pulling his phone from his pocket without shifting his gaze from hers, he flipped it open and without looking, his thumb hit a speed dial number. Figures the goon knew how to call for reinforcements by heart. "Stan. I need security now. We have a trespasser."

'Trespasser' her pretty little derriere. Reaching into her pocket, she realized she'd left her phone in the car. There was more than one way to win an argument. If it worked for tree huggers, it could work for her. Turning and stomping her way toward the truck, she could hear the man laughing, thinking he'd won. "Not on your life, buster."

Her side was beginning to hurt, but now was no time to stop. Stepping over the wood framing and the few steel rods weaved across, she could hear the guy screaming at her to get out. Instead, she stopped at the foot of the big concrete truck, set her legs slightly apart for better balance and crossed her arms. Either this truck was going to back off or she would truly be fitted for cement shoes. The worst part, if not for all the witnesses, she wouldn't put it past him to toss her into the Gulf, cement shoes and all.

CHAPTER FIFTEEN

Every impossible scenario from Tess lying on the ground bleeding internally or being rushed to the hospital to Tess buried under a mountain of concrete, clawing for air, played on a never-ending loop in his mind as he pressed harder on the gas pedal. If ever there was a day when the speed limit was taken as a suggestion not a definitive, it was now.

Flashing his ID at the construction site gate, he barely slowed long enough to ask if his project manager Teresa Gordon was there. The guy nodded and Cooper hit the gas, scanning the distance for any sign of his high school tutor. It only took a few seconds to spot the five-foot-six spitfire standing like a totem pole in front of a truck. A cement truck whose barrel had stopped spinning and was about to pour—with Tess in the way.

Unable to reach them on foot, he flew as close as he could, his hand coming down hard on the horn and staying there. All heads turned toward him except one; Tess was too busy playing a game of chicken with a cement truck.

Had she lost her mind? Bringing the truck to a halt, he threw it in park and jumped out, not bothering to turn off his engine. Running full speed ahead, he scanned the distance and had to quickly choose between the men huddled to one side and the guy driving the truck that could literally bury Tess alive in a matter of minutes. The truck won.

As loud as he could, racing to the cement truck, he shouted, "Stop!"

The driver stuck his head out of the window. "Hey, lady, get out of there."

Another voice shouted from behind Cooper, "Start pouring."

Tess didn't budge. Either she didn't hear or didn't care. And the more time he spent with her the more sure he was that she heard everyone just fine.

Running up to the truck and kicking the chute away, he ignored the bits of cement that splashed on him and Tess. The horrified look on the driver's face gave Cooper the moment he needed to turn and jump up, grab the side handle and swing the door open with one hand to yank the driver out with the other.

"Hey, man. You crazy or something?" With one leg still in the cab and the other dangling outside, the guy seemed to be both terrified and partly enraged, though Cooper was pretty sure terrified by the fury in his Cooper's eyes was the stronger of the two emotions.

"Shut it off!" Cooper growled.

"Don't you dare." The other guy who wanted the concrete poured came running up behind him. "This is private property. You have exactly one minute to get the hell out of here before I call the cops."

"Funny," Cooper faced the guy, "I was just thinking the same thing."

Growing up in the foster-care system, Tess considered herself tough. She'd taken care of herself in one way or other for as long as she could remember, but never had she been so happy to see a knight in shining armor. Still, she wasn't moving until the trucks backed off.

"I said," Cooper had the driver by the collar, "turn it off."

"That's it." The guy whose name she still hadn't learned with the foul mouth and rolled-up sleeves, flipped his phone open. "I'm calling the cops."

"Good." Cooper didn't let go of the driver. "When they get here they can escort you and your flunkies off my property."

It took a few seconds for Cooper's words to register in the mind of the jerk, but Tess recognized the second his brain computed what Cooper had said. "Your property?"

"Technically, Baron Enterprises, but since I'm Cooper Baron, why quibble over semantics."

His shoulders slumped, the guy closed his phone and nodded at the driver. "Go ahead and turn the truck around."

"You can let go now," the driver squeaked at Cooper.

Taking one step back, Cooper nodded. "First, let the lady move away." He turned and blew out such a deep breath, Tess could hear it from where she stood. "Would you please get out of there?"

Teresa looked from Cooper to the truck and back to her own feet standing between the limited rebar. "Good idea."

Moving closer, Cooper outstretched his hand and escorted her out of the foundation frame. As soon as he latched onto her, he squeezed her hand and helped her across the lumpy ground. "You okay?"

She nodded. Truth was, her heart was pounding so hard and fast she was afraid she might have a real live heart attack any minute. "I'm okay."

Helping her across the dirt, once she was out of the foundation area, he still held onto her hand. "You look pale. Are you sure? Did they hurt you?"

The concern in his eyes made her smile. "No one hurt me. I'm just not used to so much activity."

Cooper nodded, then blowing out a long slow breath, twirled her into the fold of his arms. "Please don't ever scare me like that again."

Adrenaline fading, Tess collapsed against his shoulder. "Thanks for showing up."

"Always," he practically whispered into her ear.

The truck began rolling backwards and reluctantly, Tess eased out of Cooper's arms, straightened her back, and softly repeated, "Thank you."

"Do you two need a room?" The guy who had been barking at everyone seemed a bit too cocky for someone who was about to get investigated out of business.

Cooper let go of Teresa's hand and turned to the man

standing beside him. "We're shutting everything down. Now. Our attorneys will be getting in touch with you."

"Attorneys?" The man's gaze narrowed and in a flash, as though he'd removed one mask and put on another, his expression softened and he smiled. "That won't be necessary. I'm sure whatever little misunderstanding we have can be cleared up in a few minutes."

Nodding his head, Cooper took a step back. "It's going to take more than a few minutes to clear up the issues at hand." Retaking hold of Teresa's hand, he smiled at her, then returned his attention to the guy whose name she still didn't know. "The project is officially shut down. I want everyone off the property today."

"Do you know how much all that concrete costs?" Before the man could spew more crap, Cooper cut him off.

"This conversation is over. I want everyone out of here. If necessary I can have the constable standing by to help you."

The expression on the contractor's face shifted back to the face of a junkyard dog. "We'll leave, but you will definitely be hearing from my attorneys."

With that confirmation, Cooper turned and tugged on Teresa's hand. "You're coming with me. I'll send someone for your car."

She nodded. With the mounting pain in her side and her heart rate finally slowing, she was totally on board for someone else to drive her home. The cheap car she'd bought to get around while waiting for the dumb insurance companies to come to a reasonable settlement wasn't anywhere near as comfortable as Cooper's car.

Holding the passenger door open for her, she looked at the running board and reconsidered riding home with him.

Stepping into her personal space, he turned her slightly around. "You're not okay."

It wasn't a question. "My side is a little sore."

"That does it." He bent slightly, hooked his arms under her legs and in a single move, lifted her up and into the car. "We're going back to the ranch and I'm having the doctor come check you out."

"I just over did it. That's all."

Shaking his head, Cooper set an arm on either side of her. "Do you always have to be so stubborn?"

"I'm not stubborn. I'm merely standing my ground, being assertive, all the things I learned from you and your..."

Her words drifted off as his mouth came down hard on hers. His arms wrapped around her and she fell into the kiss. All thoughts of concrete, collapses, contractors, lawsuits, and any other unpleasantries of life completely slipped away. All she knew was that she'd never felt more at home anywhere else as she did in Cooper's arms. And she'd never wanted anything as much as she wanted a life with this man. If she were honest with herself, that was probably all she'd ever wanted.

When Cooper slowly eased away, she fought the urge to whimper. "Tess?"

"Mm?" Forming a full sentence wasn't coming easily.

"This is probably neither the time nor place, but I can't help myself. Seeing you standing there with a massive truck over you, I realized something important."

Her chin dipped slightly.

"I let life distract me after you moved away. I don't want to make that same mistake. I never want to lose you again. Ever."

She blinked. Did he just say what she thought he did? Or was she actually dreaming? Had the truck dumped all that concrete on her and this was just a dying dream?

Sucking in a deep breath, he blew it out softly. "This would be a good time to say something. Hopefully not that I'm crazy and need to leave you alone."

"No," she managed to eek out. "Please don't leave me alone—ever."

A smile eased across his face. "Thank heaven. For what it's worth, I love you, Teresa Gordon."

If she was dying or dreaming, she didn't care. She'd never been happier. "And I love you, Cooper Baron. I believe I always have."

CHAPTER SIXTEEN

"Pass the rolls, please." Cooper's sister Leah plucked a roll from the bread basket.

"How many is that?" Grams stared at the nearly empty basket.

"You know I have a weakness for Hazel's honey-baked dinner rolls."

"Don't we all." Rachel stuck her arm out and grabbed one for herself.

"I saw in the paper this morning that Manning has been under investigation for some time and is now up on a list of charges as long as my arm." The Governor slathered butter on his roll. "Teresa catching him in the act of pouring recycled concrete was pretty much his nail in the coffin."

Cooper couldn't help but grin. He was so darn proud of Tess, even though at the time he wanted to kill her for facing down a greedy and potentially unpredictable scoundrel. The doorbell rang and he practically knocked his chair out from under him, pushing away from the table. "I'll get it." Tess had hoped to be at the ranch before the family sat down to Saturday lunch, but on her way out the door, her car wouldn't start. Even though Cooper's first instinct was to pick her and Emma up, Tess convinced him she'd get there faster letting roadside service get her rolling. This was the third time her cheap *for now* car had left her nearly stranded. No matter how often the dealership checked the car over, no matter how many things they fixed, she was still stranded too many times.

Flinging the door open, Tess stood with Emma in her arms. Before he could say a word, Emma flung herself at him. In the nick of time, he took hold of her before she slipped out of Tess's grip. The toddler's giggles would lift anyone's mood. Not that his mood needed lifting, he was merely a little nervous that Tess was going to be annoyed with him when she found out what he'd done.

"Gams," the little cherub called and within seconds, his grandmother was coming down the hall, arms out, ready to cradle the child. Sometimes, he forgot how old his grandparents were. The only reminder of their age was the cane his grandfather occasionally used. Though supposedly it was for balance, the old man really seemed to use it more for announcing his arrival. In the house, Cooper didn't even know where the Governor kept the darn thing.

"There's my girl." Grams embraced her in one arm, using her other hand to tickle her tummy.

As expected, Emma grinned and giggled.

Grams turned to face Cooper. "She looks more and more like you every day."

"Grams," he almost whined.

Shaking her head and swaying in place, Grams waved him off and walked away.

"Do you think they'll ever believe you're not her biological father?"

Tess leaned into Cooper as he slipped his arm around her waist and inched them down the hall. "Does it matter? When we're married, she'll be mine anyhow." He leaned in and kissed her temple.

"Someday Emma will have to know the truth."

"As far as I'm concerned, what will matter is that I'll be her daddy. It won't matter who her biological father is."

Coming to a stop, Tess turned in the fold of his arms and pushed onto her tippy toes to kiss him for real. "Just one of many reasons I love you, Cooper Baron."

He lowered his head, kept her in the circle of his arms, and decided now was as good a time as any to break the news to her. "Since you're in such a good mood, I have something to tell you."

"Shoot." She held her smile.

"Promise you won't get mad at me."

Chuckling, she lightly pecked his lips. "No promises,

but I'll do my best."

Here went nothing. Slipping his hand down to snatch hers into his grip, he turned her around and walked her back out the front door.

The frown between her brows displayed her confusion.

With a houseful of family, there were plenty of cars parked in front of the ranch. Including his gift for his fiancée. Walking through the parked cars, Tess remained quiet, her hand firmly in his. Pausing in front of the red SUV, he took in a deep breath and said a fast prayer for the umpteenth time since buying the vehicle. "What do you think?"

"Of what?"

He touched the door handle and opened it. "There's plenty of room for Emma's car seat, and another one for, well, some day, and for more people too. It has that third-row seat you said you wanted."

Her lips pressed tightly together, she stared at the car and then slowly looked up to face him. "I'm not sure I'm following. You bought a new car even though you have enough vehicles at your disposal to open your own used car lot?"

"It's not for me. It's for you."

"You bought me a car?"

Silently, he nodded.

"It's red."

"You mentioned in passing that you wished you didn't have a car the same color as everyone else in the parking lot. I might have noticed you eyeing red cars more than others."

"You noticed?" Every day this man found new ways to surprise her.

"I notice everything about you." He squeezed her hand. "Are you mad?"

"Mad? Why would I be mad?"

"Devlin says picking out a car without your fiancée is like buying a house without your wife."

"Under normal circumstances, I'd agree with Devlin, but most fiancés aren't as observant and thoughtful as you are." She ran her hand along the edge of the door. "It's beautiful."

"Go ahead. Sit inside. If you don't like it, we can pick out something else. The dealer dropped it off on approval. We can get you whatever you like if you don't want to keep this."

Shushing him, she put her finger on his lips. "It's perfect. I love it."

"Really?"

Wrapping her arms around his neck, she gave him a peck on the cheek and then spinning around, sat in the front seat. The leather seats were considerably more comfortable than her old car. From what she could see of the dashboard, this sucker pretty much came with every bell and whistle imaginable, probably more than she'd ever find the time to use. Running her fingers along the steering wheel she sighed.

Her career choices had gone very well. Teresa made a good living, a very good living, but she was always hesitant to indulge in things for herself. Especially expensive things like new cars. Slowly, she was working on letting Cooper give her things she would not get herself. At first it bothered her just a little, like the argument in the jewelry store because she didn't want the five carat monstrosity he'd wanted to give her. Instead they compromised on a single carat solitaire. Once she realized how much Cooper enjoyed giving and reminded herself that for him, buying a car was like someone else buying a pair of shoes, it became a little easier.

"Hey," Leah called loudly from the front door. "Are you planning on eating lunch with us, or are you waiting for the next millennium?"

"I guess we'd better go inside." Cooper moved aside. When she stepped out of her new car, he put his arms around her. "Do you have any idea how much I love you?"

Circling her arms around his waist, she grinned up at him. "However much, I love you more."

"That's not possible." He once again pulled her close and kissed her.

She had no idea who loved who more, but Teresa was sure of at least one thing, between them there was enough love to share of many decades to come.

EPILOGUE

"It's always so nice to see you, Emily." Devlin's grandmother never failed to smile so sweetly at Devlin's longtime friend. It almost broke his heart every time he had to explain to the older woman that he and Emily were truly just friends. Once, longer ago than he cared to remember, they tried going on a real date. Dinner, dancing, the whole shebang. At her door, he ventured for a goodnight kiss and mid lip-lock the two broke out giggling. Not quite the same as kissing your sister, but pretty darn close.

"And it's always nice to be here. You have a wonderful family." Emily shot Devlin a sideways glance. She knew how much his grandparents wanted them to get together and knew as well as he did that it would never happen.

"Isn't this a lovely party?" Leah stood beside Grams.

"Nothing is more fun than a children's birthday party. Especially the first one." Grams' gaze darted to where Elizabeth, Mitch and Gwyneth's daughter and the only Baron great-grandchild to date, was sitting on a pony ride with her mom walking at her side.

"Do those two ever let go of each other?" Devlin got a kick out of how smitten all his siblings and cousins were with their spouses, but sometimes he wondered if they hadn't just all lost their minds.

"Which two?" Eve strolled up beside him.

His cousin had a point. Looking across the lawn, Dev could spot couples circulating through the mini circus his grandmother and Gwyneth had set up for Elizabeth's first birthday. "Cooper and Tessa."

All heads bobbed. As the newest couple in the family,

they were the ones walking the closest, always holding hands, and if they needed to shift, they'd let go of the other's hand, move, and re-snatch a different hand. To Devlin it almost looked as if they were afraid if they didn't touch the other, the love of their life would disappear.

"They are cute." Eve smiled. "I always liked Tessa in high school. It was sweet the way she bossed Cooper around, and even more fun the way he'd listen."

Leah chimed in, "Some things never change."

The group chuckled, but Devlin kept his gaze on his brother. He had never considered Cooper unhappy. As a matter of fact, Cooper was the most easygoing of his siblings, but now he practically glowed from happiness. And the way Emma clung to him, anyone would think he really was her father. Though, if Devlin thought about it, being a good dad had little to do with biology and everything to do with being present. Cooper was definitely present.

"You look awfully serious." Emily put her hand on Devlin's arm.

"Just thinking."

"Still wondering if Emma is really his?"

Devlin glanced down at his friend. "No. At first I thought maybe he was just dodging reality, but considering the way things have worked out, there's no reason not to believe them. Besides, he's my brother. He's capable of many things, but he'd never outright lie to me."

"So you think," Emily teased. "You have to admit, the little one does look an awful lot like a Baron." Like Devlin, Emily kept her gaze on Cooper and Tess and Emma.

"Lots of people with blonde hair and green eyes look like us, but I know what you mean." He also had a secret. Though he had no idea why Cooper had chosen him to confide in, but Cooper and his lovely new bride had decided they wanted a sibling for Emma before she got much older, and from the tinge of green in Tessa's cheeks when she got up close and personal with the smelly donkey, Devlin had a suspicion that the mission was accomplished.

"Here they come." Emily waved at Tessa.

Hand in hand, Cooper and Tessa walked up the lawn to the terrace where Grams and the others were chatting. Halfway up the hillside, Tessa paused and seemed to be catching her breath. Yep. After watching Gwyneth practically fall asleep standing up during her first trimester, Devlin was willing to bet a hefty chunk of the Baron fortune that Emma would have a sibling in less than nine months.

Once again, they were marching up the lawn, only now Cooper had slid his arm around Tessa's middle. Whether to support her, or comfort her, or merely enjoy her presence at his side, Devlin didn't have a clue. Most likely it was a combination of all three. And the sappy grin on his brother's face told Devlin that whatever the reason, it didn't matter. What mattered was that Cooper was happier than a pig in slop. If the grin on Tessa's face was any indication, she was pretty darn content herself. Together, those two were giving off enough happy energy to light the western power grid.

"I hear there's brisket up here somewhere?" Tessa sniffed at the air like a bloodhound on the hunt.

"The Governor didn't want the grills near all these children so they're grilling on the other side of the kitchen. I'm sure the barbecue will be coming soon." Devlin kept an eye on Tessa.

Still holding her husband's hand, she continued to sniff at the air. "If you don't mind," she stepped back, slipping her hand away from Cooper's, "I think I'll go check out the food."

Cooper nodded, kissed the woman very briefly on the lips—nothing more than a peck really—and yet, Devlin could feel the heat curling his toes from five feet away.

His gaze lingering on his wife's departing back, Cooper let out a low sigh.

"Got any news for us?" Devlin spoke so only Cooper could hear. Heaven knew if his sister and cousin heard the conversation there'd be a squealing frenzy of Baron females planning the next baby shower, birthday party, and college application in one fell swoop.

Staring at his ·brother a long minute, Cooper sighed. "Maybe."

"Maybe? Either you do or you don't."

"Yes, but," Cooper shrugged, "she doesn't want to share the news till we're sure all is well."

The pull on Devlin's cheeks and the corners of his mouth had him grinning like the village fool in no time. "Man," he slapped his brother on the back, "that's great news. Really great."

A twinkle beamed in Coop's eyes and the corners of his mouth tipped upward. "It is, isn't it?"

"I'm happy for you both. Truly happy." And Devlin meant every word of it. Nothing meant more to him than seeing his family happy, not even finding a little happiness of his own. Not that he had any history worth giving a second chance. Nope, the way the family was pairing up as if Noah were building another ark, he had to accept that he may be the lone hold out for bachelorhood. And wasn't that just a shame?

MEET CHRIS

USA TODAY Bestselling Author of dozens of contemporary novels, including the award winning Aloha Series, Chris Keniston lives in suburban Dallas with her husband, two human children, and two canine children. Though she loves her puppies equally, she admits being especially attached to her German Shepherd rescue. After all, even dogs deserve a happily ever after.

More on Chris and all her books can be found at
www.chriskeniston.com

Follow Chris' Monday Blog at her website
ChrisKenistonAuthor

Follow Chris on Facebook at
ChrisKenistonAuthor

Never miss a New Release!
Sign up for News from Chris:
www.chriskeniston.com/newsletter.html

Questions? Comments?
I would love to hear from you! You can reach me at:
chris@chriskeniston.com

www.ingramcontent.com/pod-product-compliance
Lightning Source LLC
Chambersburg PA
CBHW061548310726
48972CB00008B/2657